HOW TO SUCCEED IN LIFE

WOL-VRIEY

Burning Bulb
PUBLISHING

HOW TO
SUCCEED
IN LIFE

WOL-VRIEY

Burning Bulb
PUBLISHING

How to Succeed in Life
By **Wol-vriey**

Burning Bulb Publishing
P.O. Box 4721
Bridgeport, WV 26330-4721
United States of America
www.BurningBulbPublishing.com

Cover designed by Gary Lee Vincent.

First Edition.

Paperback Edition ISBN: 978-1-964172-32-3

CHAPTER 1

It was a regular Wednesday night in the little town of Raynham, Massachusetts. A regular warm summer night.

Earlier it had rained, but now the rain had stopped and from where Gina Luz sat behind the cash register of Bundy's Pizzas, both the wet parking lot and wet road beyond it were like a huge mirror reflecting the two nearby streetlights.

"Wednesday night sucks," Gina Luz whispered.

"What was that?" Joe Bundy asked, walking in from the kitchen.

"Nothing, boss," Gina said, surprised that she'd spoken aloud.

Joe Bundy was carrying a stack of boxed pizzas, and their smell of hot pastry and delicious spicy toppings instantly injected some needed vitality into the dull restaurant ambience.

Gina checked the laptop beside the cash register to see if any new pizza orders had come in, and then she got up and moved down the front counter to help Joe sort the pizzas for delivery.

As they sorted and merged the pizza boxes according to a logical delivery sequence, and slipped them into hot bags, Gina occasionally glanced around the shop.

Tonight, there were no diners in here; all of the restaurant booths were empty. Similarly, the patio tables were all unoccupied; the night's rain was clearly responsible for this.

For several seconds, Gina stared out at the New State Highway, watching cars drive past.

The parking lot glinted wet in the streetlights, and across the highway, in front of the deli, a passing stray dog stopped to lap at a puddle. Or maybe the mutt was staring at its reflection in the water.

Weeknights like this, most pizzas are either 'to go' or home deliveries for people watching the big game on TV, Gina thought.

"Grady or Jimmy back from their last run yet?" Joe Bundy asked.

Gina shook her head. "No, they aren—" then on seeing a pair of approaching headlights turn in towards the restaurant, she shook her head again. "One of 'em just got in."

As the arriving vehicle pulled aside to the left of the parking lot, Gina squinted through the shopfront window to see who would get out of it. Both of the young men Joe was expecting drove black cars.

"It's Jimmy," she told Joe.

Joe Bundy grunted. A short while later, Jimmy Hutch pushed the glass door open and stepped in. He nodded to the boss and then headed over to the cash register.

Gina left Joe's side and went to tally the delivery receipts with Jimmy.

CHAPTER 2

Bundy's Pizzas was a family business owned by Joe Bundy and his elder sister Susan, both of whom doubled as the chefs.

The restaurant was housed in a large building that was situated along the New State Highway (aka I-44) where it ran through the south of Raynham, a single story house with a large parking lot around it.

The front half of the house was the pizza shop.

The two middle-aged siblings, neither of whom were currently married, lived in the rear half of the building.

From humble beginnings here in this same front area pizzeria, the physically large brother and sister team were steadily turning their business into a recognized Massachusetts pizza franchise.

How Bundy's pizzas had become so successful?

Joe, though a really hard worker, was hardly what anyone would call a culinary genius. However, his older sister Susan was.

Susan Bundy had created several special and seemingly irresistible pizza recipes that no one else in the Bristol County area of Massachusetts (definitely not Pizza Hut or Domino's or any other of the big-name pizza food chains) had thought up, and that was the basis of their business success.

In Massachusetts, Bundy's Pizzas already had branches further west in Milford and Webster.

(At the moment, one of Joe and Susan's concerns about their growing franchise was what they were going to do when they reached sales territories where the almost exactly named Buddy's Pizzas were sold. But that problem was still quite far in the future and geographically a thousand miles away in Michigan.)

This particular pizzeria in Raynham was kept running more out of sentiment by the owners than from financial necessity. Either of their branches in Attleboro or Taunton could easily have coped with the orders that came in, while they just laid back and soaked up the profits.

And also, Susan Bundy felt that she needed a food laboratory in which to research and perfect more pizza recipes.

Joe too, liked the idea of an ongoing tradition of pizza creation.

Joe wanted to be able to say in future: "Here, folks, right *here* is this selfsame little pizza shop, is where it all began. This is where the magic first happened; Ground Zero, Shop Number One, where the Bundy pizza empire had its deep roots. And, guys, Susan and I? We *still* own and run the darn place."

So, the Raynham Bundy's pizzeria remained open, and employed Grady Burke, Gina Luz, Jimmy Hutch, and several others.

CHAPTER 3

Jimmy Hutch departed with a fresh round of pizza deliveries, and the boss returned to the kitchen with the latest list of orders.

The mutt that had been lapping at the puddle across the highway was still there, although now it occasionally stared over at the pizza place, like it knew delicious things were happening inside the building, and was biding its time before walking over to investigate.

For a few seconds Gina heard Joe Bundy arguing with his sister about ratios of bacon and mozzarella cheese, and then the kitchen door shut off their voices and she was left alone in the restaurant.

Gina Luz was twenty-five. She'd been working here at Bundy's for two years now. She liked the job and got along well with everyone.

Gina was also currently dating Susan Bundy, a long-term relationship that was slowly becoming less pleasant and more complicated.

Susan has become really possessive all of a sudden, Gina thought with displeasure.

She checked the pizza shop's app on her cellphone, and then the laptop again.

There was an order on the laptop. She confirmed this and then phoned the boss in the kitchen to update his list. She expected pizza delivery guy Grady Burke to get back in a short while.

She laughed when she thought of Grady. He was a handsome if shy guy.

Yep, Grady clearly likes me and I like him a little, but Susan'll have a cow and a five-legged calf if I so much as wink suggestively at Grady. That'll be it for him working here and . . .

The shop phone rang and Gina stopped thinking of Grady Burke and attended to business.

She answered the phone, saying brightly: "Bundy's Pizzas. What's your order?"

"Hey, hon, just send over my Wednesday night regular."

Gina grinned on recognizing the caller's voice. "Oh hi, Mr. Harford. How's your week been?"

"Not bad so far, hon. But a hot and spicy pizza with lots of topping will make it much better and give me hope for the weekend."

"Sure thing, sir," Gina replied. "What size pizza do you want tonight—personal, medium, or large? And which toppings do you want with it?"

Mr. Harford was an old friend of Joe Bundy who was often in the restaurant itself and whom had made a tradition of ordering a Wednesday night pizza. Gina thought he sometimes came here just to stare at her breasts and those of the two waitresses. But he was a harmless enough old guy and everyone liked him.

Gina took Mr. Harford's order, hung up, and then called his order back to the kitchen also.

Outside of the pizza shop, another set of headlights had just swung their way into the parking lot.

That has to be Grady coming in. He can deliver Mr. Harford's pizzas along with some of the next batch. I noticed two addresses in that same part of town.

Gina frowned as she watched Grady get out of his delivery van and walk towards the restaurant door.

While Gina had to admit that Grady looked kind of cute in the pizza company getup of red-and-yellow shirt, black trousers and red baseball cap, with his black hair and baby blue eyes and all, he really wasn't her type of guy at all. He was too 'nice.' Gina liked more aggressive men. Not violently aggressive. But they needed to have a firm idea of what they wanted from life. And Grady Burke seemed to lack direction of that sort.

Sure, he's good-looking, but looks alone don't pay anyone's bills.

CHAPTER 4

I'll never really understand relationships in general and women in particular, Grady Burke thought while sitting in his car after his first pizza delivery. *Gina, for instance, both likes and dislikes me. Sometimes, she's almost flirtatious, and other times, it's like . . . Oh, forget it. She's dating one of the bosses and I've no intention of getting the sack.*

Grady checked his next delivery and smiled.

Okay, Mr. Harford's weekly special coming up!

He checked that Mr. Harford's pizza was the right one, and then started up the van.

The drive to Mr. Harford's house was a short one. Grady spent most of the distance ruminating on how he really didn't want to still be delivering pizzas for a living when he was forty years old.

But for the moment . . . *Well, the hours are good and the tips are great . . . sometimes . . . But . . .*

He pulled up at the foot of Mr. Harford's driveway and got out of the car. He got the pizza out of the hot bag and regarded the old man's house.

It was a compact single-story building. Exactly the sort of place that one would expect a retired widower to live in. A pleasant and regular everyday kind of residence.

And yet, for some reason, tonight Grady felt chilled being here. He tried to shake off the chill, knowing it wasn't the weather.

Something's a little off here, Grady thought as he set off up the old man's driveway.

It was a short walk to the front door, a walk that Grady had made about thirty or forty times before—Mr. Harford being *that* regular with his Wednesday night orders. But tonight, that same easy walk seemed to take ages. The imagined distance came from Grady's strange feeling of reluctance to reach the front door.

Just before he rung Mr. Harford's doorbell, Grady Burke was consumed by an almost overwhelming urge to turn around and run away, to hurry down the driveway, leap into the front of his black Toyota Camry and drive off, never to return here. He had the crazy notion that by stepping into old Mr. Harford's house tonight he would be setting in motion events that couldn't be halted.

It's not too late to back out now, he thought.

But almost like it had plans of its own, his right index finger was already pressing the old man's doorbell.

CHAPTER 5

Grady heard the doorbell chime inside the house and waited.

When, twenty seconds later, Mr. Harford hadn't come to his front door, Grady rang again.

Still, there was no reply. Once more the doorbell chimed its sweet melody, but Mr. Harford didn't come to his front door.

Grady, hot pizza in hand, became worried. Had the order been for someone unknown to him, he'd have simply marked it down as a prank order and gone off to deliver the other pizzas in his car, but this particular customer was someone well-known to him, and so Grady's sense of responsibility restrained him from leaving.

Mr. Harford is an old, old dude. What if he's suffered a stroke or coronary, or something like that? He could be dying in there while I'm ringing his doorbell!

But of course, Grady also knew that he couldn't dial for an ambulance without being sure there was an actual reason to do so.

He looked back at his car and sighed. *Somebody's pizzas are gonna be late for sure tonight!*

Then he reached out a hand to try the doorknob.

CHAPTER 6

About a second before Grady Burke's hand would have made contact with the door handle, he heard a loud click from the lock and the door opened up.

"What the . . . ?"

As the door swung inward, he stepped back in a state of alarm that was really the carried-over dread impression he'd earlier felt.

Grady's dread didn't lessen much when he saw that the foyer of the house was empty.

No, this door didn't just open itself. I'm sure old Mr. Harford opened it and ran off quickly. But why would he do that? Some kinda prank?

The door swung fully open, letting Grady properly see the interior of the house. The antechamber lighting was subdued, but brighter light shone out from deeper inside and off to the left, where the living room had to be.

"Hey, Mr. Harford, I've got your pizza!" Grady called out, while still trying to figure out how the old man, who had to be in his mid-sixties, could possibly have opened up his front door (which had clearly been locked) and then hightailed it back into the house before the door swung open.

"Mr. Harford, your pizza's here!" Grady called out again, when his first announcement got no response.

This time Mr. Harford did reply: "Oh great, son. Please come inside. I'm feeling a little indisposed, as you might be able to tell from my voice."

Grady agreed that, yes, Mr. Harford did sound a little ill; his voice was scratchy like he had a cold.

But, if he's feeling unwell, who opened his front door just now?

The original mystery was thus heightened. As far as Grady knew, the old widower lived alone, with his two daughters both residing outside of the state with their husbands.

"Come on in the house," Mr. Harford repeated, "I'll give you a good tip."

Now Mr. Harford really sounded unwell. Just now his voice had wheezed like a record slowing down. And . . . to complete that similarity, Grady now clearly heard music looping in the background, scratchy like an old vinyl LP stuck in a groove; the music was about a bar of bluegrass fiddling that kept repeating at low volume.

"Okay, sir, I'm coming in," Grady called out and stepped into the house.

As his foot crossed the threshold, he once more had that sense that he'd just set something irreversible in motion.

The feeling was so intense that for a moment after he'd stepped fully inside the building, he froze in place, and then turned to look longingly back at his car.

Then the sensation of dread vanished as abruptly as it had arrived. Grady was left feeling confused; no longer worried, and yet suspecting he had very good reason to be.

"Well, da pizzas ain't gonna deliver themselves, dude," he said aloud.

"Hey, where's my pizza, son? Hurry up, I'm real hungry in here."

"Coming up, sir!" Grady took two steps towards Mr. Harford's living room and then tripped over something on the floor.

The pizza box almost went flying out of Grady's hands and the baseball cap off of his head, but he managed to right himself in time. Then, when he was properly balanced on his feet again, he turned around for a look at what had tripped him up.

To his surprise it was a book.

But . . . how . . . ?

His confusion was twofold. First of all, Grady could have sworn that the book on the floor hadn't been there a moment ago. He could have sworn on his mother's grave to that fact.

When the door opened itself—no, no, when the door swung open . . . it DIDN'T open itself up—there was no book on the floor there.

The second puzzle (and maybe the even bigger one), was the question of *how* the book had tripped him up. It was a little book, not much larger than a pamphlet; cellphone-sized in fact and as correspondingly flat.

By all rights, I should merely have stepped on it and not noticed it at all. No way could it possibly have made me lose my balance like I just did.

"Grady, for heaven's sake, where's my damn pizza? I'm dyin' in here!"

"Oh, sorry, Mr. Harford!" The strident impatience of the request temporarily quelled Grady's puzzlement over his near fall. It honestly did sound as if the old man was dying.

Grady was about to continue his walking, when it occurred to him to take the book along to Mr. Harford. Also, that way he couldn't conceivably trip over it again on his way out of the house.

So, he bent down and picked it up.

The book was bound in pale leather and was titled in a language Grady didn't know.

On touching the book, Grady felt a moment's oddity, as though some weird connection had occurred, as if by making contact with the book he'd completed a pseudo-electrical circuit.

Then the weird feeling was gone as abruptly as it had come. Grady put the book on top of the pizza box and finally walked out of the foyer and into Mr. Harford's living room.

"Sorry 'bout the delay, sir. I was just . . . just . . . . just . . ."

Then Grady Burke stopped stuttering and just stared. He was so shocked by what he was looking at that he was completely unaware of Mr. Harford's pizza falling from his hands.

CHAPTER 7

Mr. Harford was dead. He'd clearly been murdered. In fact, this was the sort of murder that law enforcement might describe as having been carried out 'with extreme prejudice.'

Grady stared and stared. Fear spilled over him in waves as if he was taking a shower of terror.

Mr. Harford's body sat in an armchair facing his TV, which stood beside the front wall of the living room. He was dressed in a pair of shorts and a bloody tee shirt. He was also wearing socks, as if his feet had been cold.

There were two reasons why the old man's tee shirt was bloody. The first of these was because the lower half of his tee shirt had been slit up the front and a gaping hole had then been made in his belly, out of which some of his innards were dangling.

However, the main reason why Mr. Harford's shirt was bloody was because his head had been cut off, with the resultant crimson coating of both his armchair and tee shirt.

Thought mostly dried up, the spilled blood looked really icky.

Grady's breathing came hard but slow, while his mind fought to process the terrible sight before him.

Mr. Harford's head was on top of his record player. The dead man's TV was on, but silent, and he'd clearly been listening to music when he'd been killed. Beside the television was a record rack with a large collection of LPs and an old-school hi-fi system. One of those old LPs was rotating on the record player and Mr. Harford's head was rotating along with it, apparently glued in place by his blood, which seemed congealed.

The severed head was the reason the record kept on looping that single bar of bluegrass fiddling.

Mr. Harford had died with his eyes open. The look on his rotating face showed that he'd been terrified of whatever it was that had killed him. There was blood on his lips and an accusing look in his eyes. He looked as if he'd been cheated out of something; maybe even the pizza he'd been expecting.

Grady stared and stared and stared. And then finally, he got out his cellphone and called the police.

He told them what he'd just found, and then, ignoring the fallen pizza (he had no idea where the book he placed on top of the pizza box had fallen to), he walked out of the house and sat on its porch steps to wait for the police to arrive.

I don't get it, I don't get it, I don't get it, he thought over and over again, as his mind threatened to come apart in his head. *If Mr. Harford is dead in there with his head spinning around like a record, who the hell was I talking to earlier? Because that was definitely the old guys's voice that I heard coming from inside of his house.*

It was a question with no answer. No answer that made sense to Grady Burke anyway.

CHAPTER 8

The phone rang over at Bundy's Pizzas.

Gina picked up on the second ring and then with increasing surprise listened to Grady's explanation of what had just happened at Mr. Harford's house.

"Mr. Harford was murdered? That's horrible"

At first Gina found the gruesome news exciting in a macabre sort of way. It was something to shake up the boredom.

However, the longer Grady's tale went on, the more bothered Gina became.

"Oh, c'mon now," she told him after he told her he'd heard Mr. Harford—or someone at least—speaking to him from inside the house. "You must've imagined all that."

"I didn't," Grady doggedly insisted over the phone, to a background of busy-people noises.

Gina heard a guy ask: "Hey, has anyone found the old guy's heart yet?"

"Don't look like it's in here, sir," a woman replied.

"Dammit. Has to be some kinda satanic ritual," the initial speaker went on. "Those shitheads are the ones who do shit like this. We're almost certain to find pentagrams painted in his blood somewhere in here also."

They cut his heart out? Gina wondered as a fresh thrill of excitement and fear ran through her.

Grady had been silent for a while now. When he spoke again, he lowered his voice to a whisper: "Listen, I was gonna mention hearing him talking to the cops, but then I changed my mind."

Gina rolled her eyes in the empty restaurant. "Smart choice, man. They'll think you're crazy. But seriously, I think you just mentally replayed some scenario from some old scary movie you watched. You know? No way could he have called you if he's headless like you found him."

As far as Gina was concerned, Grady was simply trying to weird her out with all this talk of the dead man holding an out-of-sight

15

conversation with him. She'd already worked out how Mr. Harford had died:

At some point during the thirty minute break between when he ordered his pizza and Grady delivered it to him, some psychos broke into his house and chopped his head off . . . oh, and cut out his heart also. She shivered as an unwelcome thought occurred to her. *What if, unknown to Mr. Harford, his murderers were already inside his house before he called us.*

Suddenly she felt really unsafe.

Oh my dear God! That sort of thing could happen to anyone!

Grady hadn't said anything for a few seconds. Gina could almost see him shaking his head, while he tried to think of something else to say to scare her.

As if the circumstances of Mr. Harford's death aren't already creepy enough.

"Listen," Grady began saying, "the main reason I called is . . ."

Then something seemed to have distracted him at the murder location, because he fell silent for a few more seconds. The gap in their conversation was once again filled up by the sound of muted sirens and of people talking.

The woman who'd spoken earlier was saying: ". . . Limbs all locked up like that? Old guy must've been dead for hours."

"Yeah. Two or three at least," someone else agreed with her. "The killers could be well out of the state by now."

"So, why I'm calling in . . . ," Grady went on, but Gina didn't even hear him. Although his voice was in the foreground, a sudden and desperate need to completely track the conversation in the background made her automatically tune Grady's voice out and instead amplify what the police and forensics people were saying over there.

"Are you sure 'bout that timeline?" a third voice was asking. "This guy here who found the body says he came out here 'cos the stiff phoned in for a pizza."

"Nah," the woman replied, her voice eerily filtered through the phone. "The person who took the pizza order was mistaken. She heard the killers playing a joke on her, faking the dead man's voice. Hey, look at him, he's already frozen in rigor mortis—it normally takes a while, say three hours at the very least, for a body to stiffen up this much."

On finally completing this short segment of conversation, time froze up for Gina. All of a sudden, she felt like someone had packed her shirt with ice, going so far as to stuff ice cubes into her bra, like they were attempting to freeze her heart cold within her.

She began shivering, almost falling off of her seat as crazy thoughts filled her mind.

What the . . . ? If Mr. Harford's been dead for two hours at least, then who was it that called and ordered the pizza? But it WAS him. I'd recognize his voice any day!

"Hey, Gina, are you listening to me? Hey, Gina, are you still there?"

Gina finally acknowledged that Grady was talking to her; and that he'd apparently been telling her something all the while she'd been listening to the conversation occurring beyond him.

"Yeah, yeah, I'm here," she said quickly, trying to conceal how flustered she was. "Sorry, I missed that. Can you repeat what you were saying?"

"I asked you to tell Jimmy to come collect these remaining pizzas of mine for delivery. Either that or I'll bring them back to the shop. I'm too messed up now to handle any more deliveries tonight. It'll be a wonder if I can even drive myself home. I may need to call Kayla to come get me."

"Hold on for a moment." All business again, Gina used her phone app to made a quick check of Jimmy Hutch's present location. "Best you bring them back here . . . no, here's what you do: drive over to the top of Broadway, that's on your way home. I'll call Jimmy to meet you there and take over your deliveries."

"Thanks," Grady said, then added: "You know, I think you're right. I must've imagined all of that about Mr. Harford talking to me. Crazy when you think about it, right? He's dead. He can't be talking with his head chopped off like that."

Grady hung up. Gina put the phone back in its cradle and looked horrified.

Yeah, he's dead, and he can't be talking with his head cut off. But I heard him too, didn't I? And I'll swear on my life it was his voice I heard ordering that pizza!

CHAPTER 9

Sitting in the spacious living room of their two-story house on Baker Road, Tommy Burke listened to his son recount what had happened to him that night with growing bother.

Dammit, not again.

To Mr. Burke's mind, gruesome deaths—folks being beheaded and their hearts being stolen and all that sort of thing—weren't supposed to happen in sleepy towns like Raynham.

All of that Satanist B.S. should occur in the big cities like Boston and Springfield, even Worcester maybe. But for some reason, here in Raynham, we get more than our fair share of such craziness. And, it always seems to occur at this time of year. In the summer, when the heat needle is pushing up into the red, is when folks start turning up dead, in the nastiest of ways.

Tommy's mouth twisted up like he'd swallowed something bitter. He recalled a few years back when a trio of Satanist girls had made Raynham their kill zone. The bitches had even run over Marge Hills, daughter of a good friend of his, with their car. Marge had been pregnant at the time and those Satanist women had run her over and killed her.

Tommy sighed. *Well, the cops say that was what happened, but no one actually saw a car flatten her. According to bystanders, Marge just fell to the ground like something hit her and then suddenly there were tire tracks all over her. Crushed her head flat as a pizza.*

Ah, pizza. On remembering pizza, Tommy stared at his son Grady with some distaste.

All of that money spent on the kid's college education in Humanities and the kid can't get a job except as a pizza delivery boy.

Grady was still recounting his weird experience at the dead man's house. Tommy knew old Mr. Harford from his days on the high school PTA board. The old principal had been strict, but kind. A clean-cut, no-nonsense fellow, not the sort to mess about in any occultic shenanigans.

Most definitely not the sort of person you expect to die by having his head stuck on a turntable that's looping 'The Devil Went Down To Georgia.'

"Pops, I'll never understand why I didn't crap myself when I saw that," Grady said.

"You're constipated, that's why," said his older sister Kayla.

Tommy stared from Grady to his daughter Kayla. She saw him watching her and grinned back. Her lack of empathy told Tommy she was high again.

Tommy Burke suddenly felt a bit confused. *Where'd I go wrong? Like I didn't already have enough of a problem with Grady's lack of motivation, my older son suddenly decides that he's my older daughter.*

Anyone looking at Kayla Burke would be forgiven for thinking she'd been born that way. Though taller than the average woman, Kayla was very beautiful, the result of hours spent under the surgeon's scalpel. Most of the vestiges of manhood were gone—the body hair lasered off, the Adam's apple shaved down. As a young man, Kyle Burke had been several inches taller; while becoming female, two inches had been lost, along with quite a bit of muscle mass that had silently faded away over the past five years.

Tommy's money had paid for the transformation, of course. He hadn't minded. He was wealthier than his children imagined.

If only Kayla would get rid of her dick too, find a nice guy to marry and adopt a few kids with . . . But no, now she seems to take pleasure in taunting me with her otherness. Not to mention her perversions. And . . . and sucking dick on webcam, of course.

Tommy Burke frowned from one of his two offspring to the other, unsure which of them he was the more disappointed with, the slacker or the trans porn actress.

Maybe if the big 'C' hadn't taken Helen away like that, the kids would've have turned out better.

Nowadays, remembering his late wife was problematic to Tommy, because Kayla was almost the spitting image of her mother as a young woman. She had the same jagged looks and flawed beauty as her mother had possessed back then.

Unaware of his father's dark thoughts, Grady was telling he and Kayla about how he'd imagined he'd heard Mr. Harford asking him to come into the house.

"You didn't tell the cops that, didya?" Kayla asked with a pretty pout, while she twirled her long blonde hair around her long fingernails.

Kayla was blonde like their mother had been. Grady on the other hand, had Tom's black hair. However, both siblings shared Tom's blue eyes, eyes that were almost too blue to be natural.

"Your brother ain't dumb," Tommy chided Kayla. "He knows the cops will simply assume he hallucinated it all."

"And then test him for vaping cannabis while driving," Kayla added.

"I've no idea how the front door got opened either," Grady said, looking and speaking like he was still in shock.

Suddenly, Tommy Burke felt a great surge of sympathy for his son. Watching Grady trembling in that armchair, he understood what the kid was going through.

The kid looks miserable. Must've been sheer hell walking in on that, he thought with a grim smile.

Tommy got to his feet. "I think we all can do with a drink right now," he told his son and daughter. "You two with me on that?"

Kayla nodded. "Sure."

Tommy waited for Grady's response, but then decided Grady's silence meant consent. He walked over to the home bar on the opposite side of the living room and got down a bottle of Jim Beam and three glasses.

"It was weird all around," Grady said as Tommy returned to the others. "Even before I found the corpse. I tripped over some damn book in the front room."

"What book?" Kayla asked as she accepted a glass of whiskey from her father.

"It was so weird," Grady said. "I'd just walked in through the front door and then I tripped and almost fall and then there's this book on the floor . . . only, I'm a hundred percent certain it wasn't there when the door opened."

"Like it suddenly materialized out of nowhere?" Kayla asked. "Ugh, that's creepy."

"What did the book look like?" Tommy asked Grady as he handed him a glass of whiskey too, much more whiskey than he'd poured for Kayla. "What size was it?"

"That's the craziest thing, pops," Grady replied. "In addition to it not being there earlier, it was way too small to have tripped me up anyhow. It was bound up in soft leather and the words were in some weird language that I never saw before."

"That's creepy," Kayla repeated. "I mean, what would old Mr. Harford be doing with something like that? If it's not even in English?"

"Yep, that is creepy," Tommy acknowledged. For some reason, Grady's mentioning this book was having an odd effect on him.

"So, what did you do with it?" Kayla asked after sipping her drink. "The book, I mean."

Grady took a long gulp of his whisky before replying: "I put it on top of the pizza box. And then, when I found the corpse, I dropped them both and after that I dunno what—"

Grady stopped talking and felt his right pants pocket. The look on his face turned from upset to alarmed, and next he slid a small booklet out of his pocket.

"How the hell!?" Grady spat out, holding the book up so that Tommy and Kayla could both see it. "I'd have sworn I put it on top of the pizza box and . . . and . . ."

His sister had already snatched the book from his fingers. Tommy studied it while she did.

The kid's right; it's way too small to trip over.

The book was about the size and thickness of a cellphone. Like Grady had just told them, it was bound up in some kind of fancy leather.

"Ugh, is this animal skin?" Kayla asked as she opened the little book. "Cuz it feels like it is. And all the pages are made of the same leather." Now she had a look on her face like she'd touched something abominable; something utterly revolting.

"Here, let me see it," Tommy said and took the book from her. The moment his fingers touched the little leather-bound volume he understood the disgusted look on his daughter's face. There was something strange, strange in a bad way about this little volume that Tommy Burke now held in his hands.

Bad vibes being transmitted like germs, was the best way he could put it.

The writing on the cover of the book was in red ink, ink that looked like dried blood.

The lettering on the cover was in a language that Tommy had never seen before. It wasn't the regular Latin alphabet that most of the world used nowadays, and neither did it seem to be either Cyrillic or Arabic, Chinese, or any of the other Asian types of writing. It didn't even look like ancient runic writing.

As if reading his mind, Kayla said, "Pops, that writing looks alien—like, not of this world."

Tommy nodded. "Yeah, you're right, honey. It does."

And yet, it seemed to Tommy Burke that if he put a little effort into it, he'd be able to read the writing on the book, though he didn't know what language it was in.

Comprehension of the weird script hung at the edge of his mind like vultures circling a dying man.

In the meantime, Grady had finished up his first drink and was pouring himself another. An even more generous portion of whiskey this time.

Tommy gave his son a worried look. Grady had never been much of a drinker. But then Tommy shrugged:

Ain't every day that you see a severed head rotating on a turntable . . . or . . . find a strange book like this one.

"Pops, I agree with Grady," Kayla said. "This little book couldn't have possibly tripped him up. It's as thin as a magazine."

Tommy nodded his agreement.

"The more I look at it, the more I wonder what Mr. Harford was doing with it," Kayla added with a shiver.

Tommy didn't reply to this. He was flipping through the book's pages. Inside was more of the same, the same gibberish lettering done in the same blood-red ink and another ink that was feces-brown in color.

And Tommy was now convinced that the book was entirely made of human skin. This knowledge came from the wrongness that the little volume spilled out like water squeezed from a sponge, as if vast amounts of human agony and tears, and of suffering beyond mortal understanding, had gone into its creation.

The more Tommy stared at the pages, the more entranced he felt himself becoming. Yes, there was meaning in here, meaning that hung just on the end of cognition; waiting to be teased into his conscious mind. Tommy was certain of this.

Finally, Tommy Burke reached the end of the little book and shut it.

Tommy was barely aware of his son taking the book away from his trembling fingers.

He picked up his drink from the end table it stood on and took a sip. He felt like saying something to his two children about the book, but Kayla was pouring herself some more whiskey, and Grady was now studying the book's cover with a look of fascination on his face.

The moment dragged on. Kayla straightened up again with her whiskey, caught Tommy's eyes, and nodded towards Grady.

"He looks like he's in a trance; like he's found a new religion—the Cult of Book," she said.

"That he does," Tommy agreed.

Then Grady's eyes focused again. After shaking his head as if just realizing he'd not been himself for a while, he looked at his sister and father.

"This book is titled 'How to Succeed in Life,' " he said, wagging the skin-bound volume in the air at them.

Understandably, both Tommy and Kayla gaped at him.

"Huh?" Kayla said. "You can read the writing on it?"

Grady shook his head. "I still can't. But that's what's written on the cover—'How to Succeed in Life.' "

"Son . . ." Tommy said slowly, not liking this one bit, because he felt Grady was either getting drunk, or was losing his mind, "if you can't read the words, how can you understand what they mean?"

Grady shrugged. "I dunno, but that's what it says. I just concentrated deeply on the writing and all of a sudden its meaning was in my mind."

He offered the book to Tommy. "Here, pops, you try it."

Remembering how he'd felt while flipping through the book, Tommy Burke shook his head. "Uh uh, son, not happening."

Grady offered the book to Kayla instead: "Sis?"

She shook her head even more emphatically than their father had. "Me either, dude. Your weird book is entirely your property and your responsibility." Then her expression turned sober. "But, don't you need to turn that in to the cops anyway? Crime scene evidence?"

"Yeah," Tommy quickly agreed with her, suddenly desperate to get Grady's creepy find out of their house. "It might be a clue in Harford's murder."

Grady's face creased up while he thought about it. "Yeah, maybe, but I doubt it."

"Why'd do you say that?" Tommy asked him.

"I dunno," Grady replied, while sliding the little volume back into his pocket. "I just have a conviction that the police won't be able to make head or tails of this book either." Then he frowned. "I've also got a strong conviction that I was *meant* to find it; that the book *wanted* me to find it."

"Okay, now you're sounding drunk," Tommy replied. He glanced at the clock opposite them all, near the living room TV, and then waved his drink at the others. "We can decide on it tomorrow. It's way past midnight now and I need to get to bed."

"Me too," Kayla agreed, after draining her glass of alcohol. "I've got a busy schedule tomorrow."

With misgivings concerning what his daughter's 'busy schedule' entailed, Tommy Burke picked up the whiskey bottle, nodded goodnight to his two grown-up children, and headed for his bedroom at the rear of the house.

Tommy told himself that the reason he was taking the whiskey with him was to prevent Grady from drinking any more of it tonight.

However, the real reason for Tommy's doing so (seeing as even if he deprived his son of this bottle of hard liquor, the living room still had a fully stocked bar), was that he wanted to get a little drunk himself.

Grady's creepy find had unsettled him more than he cared to admit to himself.

As he walked past the kitchen and entered the ground floor hallway, Tommy recalled the 'badness' he'd felt seeping from the skin-bound book's pages, like germs of death and destruction infecting his home and corrupting the lives of his entire family.

Grady had better get rid of that thing fast. Either he throws it away or hands it over to the cops or whatever. But he needs to get it out of my house!

On that thought, Tommy Burke pushed open his bedroom door and then poured himself a stiff whiskey.

Drinking it made him feel a lot better.

CHAPTER 10

The next morning Tommy ate breakfast with Kayla, Grady having already left home.

In the Burke household this was the normal morning routine. Tommy and Kayla both worked at home and as such got up late every day.

Today they were having breakfast at 10.30 a.m.

Kayla's remodeling into a feminine role in their home was a total one. With passable results she cooked all of their meals and also cleaned the house. Many times while watching her bustle about doing one thing or the other, Tommy felt very confused as to whether there had ever really been a young man named Kyle Burke. It seemed as if his first child had always been a daughter.

This morning at breakfast, neither Tommy nor Kayla mentioned yesterday night.

Indeed, as she always did, Kayla spent most of the meal staring at her cellphone, making exclamations of surprise and posting comments, and taking several selfies.

By this morning, Tommy himself had more or less forgotten the book Grady had brought home with him last night. Tommy's main concern this morning was surviving the raging hangover that last night's drinking had left him with.

Three cups of black coffee so far weren't helping and he kept glancing over at the home bar's liquor cabinet, longing for an alcoholic pick-me-up.

But I got work to do this morning. I can't start drinking this early.

Kayla, however, seemed none the worse. She looked as fresh, as effervescent, as ever.

But then she's both decades younger than I am and didn't drank anywhere near as much whiskey as I did.

"Okay, pops, I'm heading upstairs," Kayla said, pushing back her chair and getting up from the breakfast table.

She walked over to him and kissed him on the cheek. This physical contact with her was something that he enjoyed, but which also made him feel uneasy because she looked so much like her late mother.

"Just leave the breakfast things on the table when you're done eating and I'll clear them later," Kayla told him. "But for now, I've gotta get ready. I'm expecting some visitors soon and I gotta get set up before they get here. I'd planned to do it last night, but then we had all that talk about Mr. Harford's gruesome death."

Tommy grinned at her. "Okay, honey. Have fun today."

She giggled. "Oh, I will, daddy, I definitely will."

Tommy watched Kayla walk off with misgiving, knowing that the visitors she'd referred to were porn stars like herself.

And I, who know this, have just wished her a happy time getting her ass stretched with eggplants or whatever.

He frowned. Sometimes Tommy wished Kayla had remained Kyle. But, because of her striking resemblance to her mother Helen, her transformation had brought Tommy a sort of healing, an almost spiritual feeling that Helen hadn't left them for good.

The downside of this was that Tommy was now in the strange situation of watching his young 'wife replacement' constantly committing 'adultery' with strangers.

Strange but true.

If only she'd stop doing that porno and webcam thing, he thought with another loud sigh. *It'd be better then, much better.*

But Kayla had already made it very clear that porn was what she wanted to do.

"Doing it makes me feel complete, daddy," she'd told him.

"Honey, you've got a Bachelor degree in Communications," Tommy had protested. "Use it for something."

"*I am* using it for something, daddy," she'd told him. "That's why my webcam feeds are so good. You should read the comments I get."

Tommy wasn't about reading those comments. He'd accepted defeat.

She ain't doing it for the money—we've sufficient of that. Either she's doing it cuz lots of other trans women are, or my daughter Kayla is very insecure and wants the validation of her femininity that having lots of fans and followers on OnlyFans gives her, Tommy told himself, for the nth time.

A bitter pill to swallow, of course, but one played the hand life dealt them.

Tommy ate some more buttered toast, drank another mug of black coffee and then heard the sound of a car pulling up outside his house.

He quickly got to his feet. He never felt comfortable meeting the people who'd shortly be having sex with his daughter on camera.

After a glance at the stairs these visitors would soon be climbing to Kayla's upstairs bedroom, Tommy Burke hurried off to his office before the doorbell rang.

CHAPTER 11

Once he was safely in his office, and with the door closed so that he couldn't overhear any of Kayla or her visitors' conversations, Tommy Burke sat down at his laptop to get some work done.

O.K., now what are today's tasks?

He opened up his emails to see what Marko Velli wanted from him today.

***

For most of his life, Tommy Burke had worked in retail for various supermarkets. In his younger years he'd been driven to succeed for the good of his family, and had slowly risen up to a managerial position.

However, Helen's death had knocked all of the wind out of Tommy's sails, and left him drifting aimlessly. A lot of that burning ambition he'd previously had had been because he'd wanted to give Helen all of the good things of life; and now that she was no more, what point was there in driving himself so hard?

When Helen died, both of their sons were already in college and would soon be making their own way in the world.

After Helen's passing, Tommy had coasted on for a while, still doing his job well, but really just doing enough to remain employed.

(Relationship-wise, Tommy's life now consisted mainly of meetings with escorts in motels when the urge for sex came upon him. Initially, Tommy simply hadn't wanted the complications of introducing other women to his sons. But over time, hiring prostitutes had become the norm in his life.)

Now, at this point when Tommy's life seemed to have stalled for good, two unexpected things had happened to him.

Firstly, this was the period where Kyle, who up to that point had seemed to be a normal heterosexual young man, had suddenly announced that he was in the wrong body.

Seeing no point in arguing about it and thereby driving the young man away from home or possibly even to suicide, Tommy had supported Kyle's gender transition with all of the necessary funds.

The cost of Kyle's becoming Kayla would have been quite a drain on the family's accounts, except for the second thing that had happened.

Now, Tommy Burke had been fooling around with crypto currency for years. Though he hadn't made a financial killing with it like some others, he understood all of the ins and outs of crypto trading and what could be done with it.

Most importantly, Tommy had worked out how to move money about in complete secrecy via crypto platforms and tumblers and wallets. Sure, it wasn't like he had any money to move anywhere illegally, but still, it was fun and empowering knowledge to have at his fingertips.

This latter detail (i.e. Tommy's not having any money to move about secretly) had changed three years ago, on Kayla's twenty-fifth birthday.

The details went like this: The birthday bash had been held in the Burke house, which was very large, and all of Kayla's friends, both the regular people and the sex freaks, were all cordially invited.

Among the attendees was Danny Foster, whom Tommy knew as a drag performer under the name Dierdre Fabulous. Danny Foster had been accompanied by his boyfriend Sluggo Lakes, who Tommy didn't know, but whom Kayla later explained was a mobster.

During the course of the evening, Tommy and Sluggo (who were possibly the only people in attendance who weren't stoned on pot or something harder) had gotten to talking, and their talk had gotten around to money: how to make it, how to save it, how to invest it, and if necessary, how to hide it. Tommy, under the influence of alcohol, had jokingly mentioned to Sluggo that he knew how to anonymously move large amounts of currency around using cryptocurrency platforms. Sluggo had gotten a strange gleam in his eye then that Tommy hadn't noticed.

Anyway, a few days later, Tommy Burke had gotten a visit at home from both Sluggo Lakes and a stocky middle-aged man whom Sluggo had introduced as his boss, Marko Velli.

Sluggo had explained to Tommy that Mr. Velli had lots of illegally-acquired money scattered around the world that he needed to bring back home to the USA, and that if Tommy helped Marko convert this illegal money to legal money, Tommy would be paid handsomely, but that if Tommy didn't help Marko Velli fix his money problems, Tommy would most likely wind up in the nearest patch of Atlantic Ocean (which would most likely be Cape Cod Bay, a mere 25 miles away) wearing a concrete hat, a concrete necklace, and concrete boots.

It was the typical mob 'offer you can't refuse,' and understanding this, Tommy Burke hadn't refused, and that was how he'd quit working in supermarket retail and begun laundering money for the Boston mob instead.

And that led up to the here and now.

***

Tommy's work for the Boston mob went something like this:

A patriotic American (even if he was a violent criminal kingpin) Marko Velli wasn't actually adverse to paying taxes to the IRS.

However, he was extremely adverse to them investigating and discovering the source of his illegal gains, particularly since Marko himself wasn't exactly sure that some of his revenue wasn't being generated by a child prostitution ring somewhere in Southeast Asia.

(Yes, Marko knew his criminal partners had prostitutes working out there, but said partners were excessively vague about the ages of some of the 'hired' sex workers.)

So, not desiring to run foul of American law enforcement, Marco's solution was to clean up the dirty money via Tommy's crypto-laundry route and then invest this clean money into a famous South Korean electronics and cellphone manufacturing giant (aka Samsung) which then paid him handsome dividends that the IRS could safely tax.

For Tommy's part in this roundabout fix, he was now worth over a million dollars, all of it legally paid to him by a Thai company (not the prostitution guys) for 'financial consultancy expenses.'

CHAPTER 12

Tommy got down to work, loading up his forex tracking apps, his banking apps and opening up his crypto platforms and wallets.

Marko Velli had a million dollars in opium-trafficking profits that he needed to move out of Hong Kong and Macau without their respective governments wising up to that fact.

After dissolving the dirty funds into crypto, tumbling them like dice through the Dark Web and finally pulling them out again as clean as ice cubes, Tom had three options of where to put them. He could either invest the money in Samsung, put it in a Swiss bank, or invest it in a French arms company.

After a little thought he chose the French weapons manufacturers. War was big business at the moment, and that trend seemed likely to escalate.

Thirty minutes later, Marko Velli was a part-supplier of the next batch of anti-aircraft missiles that NATO would be supplying to Ukraine. An irony if there ever was one, as Marko was vocally sympathetic to the Russian side of that violent territorial argument.

Smiling at the joke he'd just played on his mobster boss, Tommy got up and paced around his office for a while.

Using one bedroom as office and the other for sleeping, Tommy Burke occupied the two bedrooms at the rear of his house on the ground floor.

The three bedrooms on the upper floor, he'd left to his son and daughter.

The reason for this arrangement was simple: This way Tommy was as far away as possible in his house from the noises of Kayla's endless OnlyFans and Just For Fans copulations.

Once Tommy shut the doors of his own rooms, he was well isolated from all the carnal grunts and moans that filming transgender porn generated.

Now, Tommy walked over to the north window of his office, and stared out at his backyard. There was little to see out there; just lush grass and trees, and soon Tommy's gaze swept left instead.

Over there the view was more rewarding, as he caught a glimpse of his hot divorcee neighbor Annie Smith drying her laundry. Annie's halter top and shorts presented a great view of her sweet body, and suddenly Tommy wished he had a woman in his arms again.

Then, recalling his last intimate experience with a woman, he sighed loudly.

Restricting one's sex life to prostitutes was bound to produce some strange encounters, and Tommy had had a few of those.

Tommy laughed at those memories. Then he frowned and shook his head.

His last encounter with an escort, which had occurred two months ago, had been bittersweet. The young woman, Anita, had been attractive and pleasant enough, and the sex had been satisfactory, but afterwards, when Tommy had fallen asleep in their motel room, she'd absconded with his wallet.

Tommy shook his head at the memory. *Okay, so there was three hundred bucks extra in there after I'd paid her. She could've just taken the money and left my wallet. What the hell did Anita want with my damn driver's license? My credit cards too, but as far as I can tell she's not even tried to buy anything with the cards.*

Tommy hadn't reported the theft to law enforcement.

What would I say? Officer, the hooker I hired ripped me off?

Instead, he'd called her a few times to try to get his stuff back, but then she'd blocked his number.

Other than from a desire to do something mean to him, Tommy still couldn't understand why Anita had stolen his wallet.

That experience with Anita had soured Tommy where hiring escorts was concerned.

But now, as Tommy watched his attractive neighbor turn back into her house, the need for a woman grew strong in him, and he knew it wouldn't be long before he dialed up another escort.

Tommy crossed back to his work desk and seated himself again.

Alright, back to work, he told himself, tapping away his laptop screensaver, *Sluggo was complaining that their Philippines project is—*

And then, on picking up his cellphone to check something, Tommy Burke shivered.

When he'd gotten up to stretch his legs, he'd left a banking app in focus on his cellphone.

Now, however, he was staring at a popup banner that flickered in bright colors the message: 'HEY, TOMMY BURKE, DOWNLOAD YOUR FREE COPY OF 'HOW TO SUCCEED IN LIFE!'

How to Succeed in Life? Wasn't that the supposed name of that weird leather book that Grady came home with last night?

The book advertised on his phone appeared normal though. Its cover art depicted a smiling young executive woman descending a flight of stairs with a laptop in her left hand.

I ain't got time for this nonsense, Tommy told himself, realizing this was just another self-help book promo.

He tried to click away the intrusive banner, but the window didn't close. He tapped the phone screen several times, with the same lack of a result.

Finally realizing that the only way he'd be able to get back to his bitcoin apps was to download the offered book, Tommy did so.

I hope this thing ain't carrying any phone viruses.

'THANKS!' the banner announced and vanished.

Tommy heaved a sigh of relief. Then he noticed that, as if it were an app, the book seemed to have automatically installed itself on his phone.

But . . . why does the thumbnail image now look like the book Grady brought home? Tommy wondered as a fresh shiver ran through him.

Acting against his better judgement, Tommy tapped on the creepy book/app.

There was a flash of 'black light,' a moment when it felt as if the world had been split apart around Tommy Burke and then reassembled, and then, suddenly, Tommy wasn't holding his cellphone in his hand any longer, but instead was holding something like the skin-bound book Grady had brought home last night.

Tommy's shock was so great that he immediately dropped the book. Then he backed away fast, only stopping when his back hit the bookcase by the north window.

What the . . . ? What the . . . ?

Because now, Tommy could clearly see that his cellphone was lying on his desk beside his laptop. And the skin book with the strange lettering on its cover *still* lay on the blue rug where he'd just dropped it.

And Tommy knew, he knew beyond any shadow of a doubt, that this book, this book that he'd just 'downloaded' from *somewhere*—but where the hell had it just come from?—was an *exact* copy of the book that Grady had brought home from Mr. Harford's house last night.

Tommy was certain of that: that this wasn't that same book, but a copy; manufactured, printed, copied, whatever; made by the same people.

Tommy now felt very afraid. He tried to find a logical explanation for what had just happened, but his best mental efforts came up blank.

That book came out of nowhere! he thought finally while slowly making his way back over to his work desk.

The closer Tommy got to the book, the more bothered he felt, but also the more curious.

Before he realized what he was doing, he'd picked it up again. Once more he had that creepy sensation of an invisible infection—paranormal germs from an eldritch festering orifice—oozing from its tanned skin covering to infect him and all that he held dear.

But now, Tommy's curiosity linked him to the book the way a magnet attracts metal. The world faded away from around him, until finally existence consisted solely of the flimsy skin volume his fingers gripped.

"How to Succeed in Life."

Not understanding how he could translate a language he'd never seen before, Tommy nonetheless read the words smoothly off of the cover of the book.

And then he opened it up and began reading its content.

And its content was terrible indeed.

Truly, the book promised success in life, but at a staggering and an evil cost.

Tommy felt horrified by what the book demanded of its readers. And yet, he also desired that ultimate success—the surpassing acme of human achievement—that the book promised to those who did what they read in its pages.

CHAPTER 13

While her father trembled in fear because of the strange book that he'd somehow 'downloaded,' Kayla Burke was filming that day's sex uploads.

"Hey, fans, this is your number one trans girlfriend fap2kayla69!" she told the cameras brightly.

This morning, two friends were helping Kayla film. Mr. and Mrs. Stainless Strange (or just 'Strange') were an actual married couple, with the wife being transgender. Both husband and wife were dressed in head-to-toe black latex with the crotches of their costumes unzipped to reveal their erect penises. Occasionally the couple passed a THC vape pen between themselves.

"Yeah, and assisting me today are yours truly—Mr. and Mrs. Stainless Strange!"

This announcement prompted the latex-clad couple to wave at the cameras.

Kayla herself was naked except for her makeup and a pair of pink crotchless panties. She was sitting at the foot of her bed and playing with her breasts. Her penis was hard. Occasionally, she dropped a hand from fondling her breasts and tugged on her erection instead.

The video camera filming Kayla was on a tripod.

"Okay, baby, that's nice," Mrs. Stainless Strange whispered, moving the camera forward a little. "Go on, go on."

"So today, I'm gonna explore the sexual benefits of fruit," Kayla announced. "Everyone knows fruit is good to eat—fruits are full of vitamins and minerals and stuff like that. But . . . do you guys also realize fruit is good to fuck?" Kayla giggled loudly. "Yeah, everyone, fruit is good to have sex with too. For one thing, fruit doesn't give you STDs. Also, fruit never has headaches or limp-dick syndrome. Best of all, fruit doesn't require batteries to operate."

On a cue from his wife, Mr. Strange placed a tray of fruit on the bed beside Kayla, who now stopped looking at the video camera and examined what was on the tray instead.

"Well, well, what have we here?" Kayla picked up a large eggplant. "This looks just like a butt plug, doesn't it? And you guys all know that purple is one of my favorite colors. And next to the eggplant we've got a fabulous cucumber." Here Kayla paused and looked in mock horror at Mr. Strange. "Darling, why are they all so big? Are you trying to prolapse me? Still angry that I came in your eyes last night?"

She giggled and wagged the massive cucumber (it really was BIG) at her internet audience (most of her subscribers weren't online yet; this video would be edited and uploaded later). "But, no worries. My back door has handled bigger challenges in my time. Yeah, guys, one more benefit of fruits—they don't go soft on you after they come."

"And cut!" Mrs. Strange said, with a chopping gesture of her right hand.

"Guys, these fruits are huge," Kayla said worriedly once the camera was no longer filming her. "That cucumber will split my ass wide open."

"Relax, Kayla," said Mr. Stainless Strange. "You won't need to demonstrate with those. Mrs. Strange will dildo herself with the big cucumber and the eggplant."

"Yes, I will," his wife agreed, pinching her nipples to harden them. "For you, the high point of this morning's filming is when you fuck the banana."

Kayla nodded. Fucking the banana was a strange thing that Mr. and Mrs. Strange had suggested. Usually, people inserted bananas into their bodies for sex, but the kinky couple had realized that it was possible to do it the other way also. If you hollowed out a banana—it had to be a large one though—you had a natural masturbation sleeve, all lubricated and ready to penetrate.

"Yeah," Kayla said, with a nod. "The guys are certain to go crazy for that, particularly when I come inside the banana skin and pour the come into your husband's open mouth."

Mr. and Mrs. Stainless Strange both nodded. Mr. Strange sucked on his THC vape and then blew the smoke at Kayla's face so she could share his high. Kayla sucked in the heady fumes and grinned back at them.

"Using the banana like that will drive your subscribers wild," Mrs. Strange agreed. "And meanwhile, I'll be sucking Mr. Strange off, and getting him to come too." She shrugged. "Or maybe I'll fuck his ass, if that looks better for the fans."

Not for the tenth or even twentieth time, Kayla was struck by how weird the pair of them were.

I've never once seen either of their faces. They always arrive here dressed like this, and we fuck and then they depart to the devil knows where they live . . . until next time.

But Mr. and Mrs. Stainless Strange were so good on camera that her fap2kayla69 fans keep requesting for them to return in her videos.

But . . . I don't even know their real names. They refer to themselves, either as 'my husband' and 'my wife,' or as 'Mr. Strange' and 'Mrs. Strange.' Wow, how strange is that?

Kayla admitted that the pair were quite harmless. They were just ridiculously kinky. Mrs. Strange had huge breasts and a larger penis than her husband, and kept coming up with weird sexual scenarios.

Like the time when they'd all ejaculated into a bottle of champagne and then auctioned the bottle off to the highest bidder.

There was a lot of semen mingled in with that wine, because Shannon and Mira were part of that orgy also—damn, afterwards it seemed like there were worms in that bottle.

She giggled. *And someone actually paid us $3000 for that bottle of tainted bubbly.*

The winner of the auction had been a man who wanted to give his girlfriend 'something special' for their first anniversary, and thought blended wine and come would do the trick.

Being a webcam girl definitely beats when I was doing the 9-to-5, Kayla thought contentedly.

She liked the work hours and she liked the money, and she *loved* the fact that she was adored by the men and women who subscribed to her and masturbated to her and held her as an icon.

Mr. Stainless Strange was lying back on Kayla's bed, vaping away and staring at his cellphone. His penis was stiff in his crotch, courtesy of the boner pills they'd each taken.

Meanwhile, Mrs. Strange was bent over Kayla's bedroom table, pulling something out of her handbag.

Mrs. Strange had a fat ass; like someone had maybe found an extra ass discarded somewhere and glued it onto the one she already had. With her latex catsuit unzipped at the crotch, her balls swung as she searched through her purse and her anus winked invitingly at Kayla.

Kayla tapped Mr. Strange on his feet.

"I wanna fuck your wife," she told him. "Film us on your phone."

"Okay!"

Kayla got up to her feet and walked over to Mrs. Strange and knelt behind her.

"Oooh nice, darling!" Mrs. Strange moaned when Kayla began licking the crack of her ass.

Once Mrs. Strange was wet enough, Kayla slid her erection into her.

Yeah, she's definitely got enough space in here to park that massive cucumber, Kayla gasped as she began moving, forcing the other trans woman down flat on the table. *And the eggplant too . . . and the banana!*

Mr. Strange stood beside them, filming it all on his cellphone. Kayla reached for his penis and began to masturbate him.

Then her eyes fell on an unfamiliar book on her table.

What is Grady's creepy book doing in here? she wondered.

But despite her surprise, she didn't stop making love to Mrs. Strange, who at that moment switched their positions and took Kayla's organ in her mouth instead.

For some reason, Kayla's eyes remained fixed on the indecipherable script on the cover of the little skinbound volume. While Mrs. Stainless Strange sucked on her penis, and her image was sucked into the cellphone in Mr. Stainless Strange's hands, Kayla was sucked into those indecipherable words, which strangely, now began making sense to her.

Yeah, Grady was right, Kayla realized as she pulled out her penis from Mrs. Strange's mouth: *this funny book actually is titled 'How to Succeed in Life!'*

She decided she'd check it out further after her sex session.

Then she forgot the book altogether and relaxed and ejaculated on Mrs. Strange's latex-masked face, emptying her balls in 4K resolution for her OnlyFans subscribers.

CHAPTER 14

"You know, Grady," Joe Bundy said. "If I were a bad boss, I'd insist that you pay for that pizza you forgot at old Harfords."

Grady said nothing.

Then Joe laughed. "Nah, kid, I'm just kidding ya. Stuff that nasty requires bad jokes to prevent you going into shock."

Grady nodded at his boss. He, Joe Bundy, and Joe's sister Susan were out at the front counter of the pizza shop, checking inventory before they opened for the day.

Joe and Susan Bundy were alike as peas in a pod: two grossly overweight late-thirtyish people with a similar pleasant disposition. Brother and sister both had short brown hair, grayish eyes, and enough excess adipose weight between them to make two more regular-sized people.

Grady often thought that if the saying 'You are what you eat' had any truth to it, then Joe and Susan Bundy were both comprised mostly of ham and bacon and mozzarella cheese and spices and anchovies and sun-brown crusts and tomatoes and everything else that went into their pizzas.

The bosses had interrogated Grady in depth about what he'd found last night at Mr. Harford's house.

Joe had seemed vaguely thrilled by the macabre details of the murder, but Susan was clearly horrified by them.

"I don't see Gina around anywhere," Joe told his sister. "Where is she? Still asleep in your bed?"

(Though Gina had an apartment of her own across town, she spent most of her nights here with Susan.)

Susan shook her head. "Her roommate Cherry took ill overnight, so she had to go drive her to the hospital. She'll be back soon."

CHAPTER 15

Unfortunately for Grady, today he had the 11 to 5 shift.

On waking up, he'd felt so shell-shocked that he'd smoked one of Kayla's THC vapes before heading for work. Of course, Grady knew that driving under the influence of marijuana was a criminal offence, but he'd been unable to think of another satisfactory way to cope with today.

After arriving at work, Grady had hit the vape tube a few more times before work began.

Now Grady felt mellow. His only worry was that someone would catch him vaping and label him a douchebag.

Mr. Harford's murder floated around the edges of his mind like a headless angel.

"Boss, can I have the day off?" Grady asked Joe Bundy. "I'm still very shaky from last night."

All Grady really wanted to do today was get home, get stoned or drunk, and channel-surf through the hours till nightfall, when he was supposed to meet up with his bestie Ricky.

Grady would've have called that meeting off also, but Ricky had been telling him about his hot new girlfriend Molly, and he wanted Grady to meet Molly tonight.

Grady had told Ricky about Mr. Harford's murder. If possible, he intended to avoid discussing it further tonight.

Joe shook his head at Grady's request. "No can do, kid. You're late to the absence party. Megan called in sick this morning, so if I let you go too, who's gonna deliver my pizzas for me?"

Susan Bundy smiled sympathetically at Grady. "Joe's too fat to fit behind the wheel of his own truck or I'd say that he deliver his own pizzas today while I handle all of the baking."

Then Susan brightened up. "Hey, here comes Gina now," she said with a look of love on her face.

Grady looked out the shop window and saw Gina Luz's red Subaru rolling into the parking lot.

CHAPTER 16

"Creepy, that's what it was," Gina told Grady once their bosses had left them alone at the front counter. "I know I earlier gave you a hard time about dead Mr. Harford speaking to you from inside his house, but I'll swear in court if I have to that he's the one who ordered the pizza you delivered."

Gina Luz had spent a good amount of the night pondering this. The question had distracted her during lovemaking with Susan to the point where she'd needed to fake her orgasm. And afterwards, with Susan Bundy snoring gently beside her, Gina had replayed her conversation with Mr. Harford over and over again and again and again.

This morning she was no closer to an answer than she'd been the night before.

Gina studied Grady's face for signs of shock. On close inspection, his eyes seemed a little glassy, but that was all.

"You don't seem much the worse for wear today," she finally observed.

A furtive look came into Grady's eyes and he glanced around like a criminal. Then he slipped a hand into his jacket and pulled out a silver tube. "THC—the oxygen of champions," he told Gina, once she'd realized he was showing her an e-cigarette. "The only way I'm gonna make it through today."

"You're gay now?" Gina asked with a smile. "That explains why I haven't seen you with a girl in ages."

"Stop pushing stereotypes. Just cuz I vape, it don't mean I'm gay." Grady frowned. "Actually, the vape pen belongs to Kayla. She considers them an essential fashion accessory."

Gina grinned broadly now. "See? Dude, you just defeated your own argument."

"*You're* gay, aren't you?" Grady countered.

Now it was Gina's turn to glance furtively around. "Nope, I'm not," she finally whispered to him.

She felt amused when Grady looked confused. It was a definite step up from her own confusion about her possible impossible delusion.

"But . . . you and Susan are . . ." Grady said slowly.

"Lovers," Gina agreed. "She loves me and I love her money."

Grady nodded sagely to this. Now that Gina knew he was tripping out on Planet Reggae, she doubted that he got the proper implications of her confession.

"Tell anyone what I just told you and your balls will end up sliced into one of our pizzas," she warned Grady, who merely nodded back. In fact, Grady looked so mellow, Gina wondered how the hell he'd manage to deliver any orders today.

But then, he may not need to, she reasoned. *Afternoon shift is sometimes as slow as a snail.*

"Hey listen," Gina said. "We're getting sidetracked here. The problem of the hour isn't my morals, but how could Mr. Harford have been dead for at least three hours by the time he phoned here?"

Grady shrugged. "I'd need to be Steven Hawking or Carl Sagan to answer that. You know, quantum physics and time-differential theory?"

Gina rolled her eyes at him. "Don't you rather mean Tyler Henry or the Psychic Twins?"

CHAPTER 17

Ricky Lawson was tall, handsome, and muscular, with long dark hair and eyes the color of tree bark. He and Grady had been best friends for several years now, starting from when they'd both worked at the Walmart Supercenter down on Broadway.

Tonight Grady was meeting Ricky at Ricky's apartment, a half of a duplex that he rented from the old couple who lived next door.

"Hey, bro, you look wasted," Ricky told Grady at his front door.

"You don't know a quarter of it," Grady responded as he stepped into the house.

"And this is Molly," Ricky said, when they got into his living room. "Molly Woods."

"Hi," Molly waved from her place on the living room couch. Molly Woods was extremely pretty and busty, with hair confused between blonde and brunette. Grady tried to make up his mind if she was more pretty than busty or vice versa. He was left with half a boner and a hung jury.

Grady sat and Ricky handed him a can of beer. "You seem like you could use it."

Grady nodded back. "Dude, you don't wanna know how my day's been."

"I won't ask."

Rick crossed the living room to sit beside Molly on the couch. Watching them snuggle up close to each other, Grady wondered where his own love life had vanished to.

My love life is likely waiting for me to find the right girl again.

"Ricky told me that you saw a murder last night," Molly said.

Grady sighed. "That, I wish I could unsee." He recounted the details of the killing. Then, after Ricky got him another beer, he added the weird stuff that had accompanied it.

"Damn, dude. For real?" Ricky asked afterwards.

"Yeah, yeah. Gina was close to a freak-out this morning, and *she* didn't see the head revolving on the old-school record player."

During Grady's tale, Molly had been largely quiet. At points her eyes had widened with horror and at others she'd laughed in amusement, but for the most part she'd just listened.

"That book you found," she said now in wowed tones, "What did you do with it?"

"I brought it with me." Grady reached into his jacket and pulled it out.

"Lemme see it," Molly told him, gesturing at him to bring it over.

Grady got up, walked over, and handed the book to her.

"Wow, this is weird," Molly said after studying it for a few moments. "It's great!"

"What do you mean 'it's great?'" Ricky asked. Ricky had a worried look on his face. He sighed at Grady.

"Molly used to work for her aunt, who's a medium," he explained. "She's into weird occultic stuff."

"Not really," Molly immediately countered. "I used to be into the occult, but not so much anymore. However, this book reminds of way back then."

Grady nodded. His eyes were fixed on Molly, because Molly's eyes were fixed on the book. Indeed, since he'd handed it to her, she'd not stopped staring at it, as if . . . Grady knew what she was experiencing— the world seeming to shrink to nothing around her until the book was the entire universe.

"I'm certain this is human skin it's made of," Molly said after a while, her voice seeming to come from a distance. "It's got the right feel and texture."

"It's titled 'How to Succeed in Life,'" Grady said.

"Yes," Molly instantly agreed, without looking at him and while turning over a pale leather page. "That's what it says on the cover."

She was still staring at the book as if hypnotized, and her boyfriend now gave Grady a worried look.

"How can you both know what's written on it?" Ricky asked. "This writing looks like no language I've ever seen before."

"Don't ask me," Grady replied. "I don't understand it either. No, I do. I think once you concentrate on it, the book explains itself to you."

"Yes, it does explain itself to you," Molly agreed in her far-off voice and with that spaced-out look in her eyes and her gaze totally riveted within the book's pages. Grady also noticed that she'd begun breathing faster.

"C'mon, both of you, that's crazy," Ricky said. "It isn't a damn Kindle or a cellphone. It's a paperback. Paperbacks don't talk."

"Yep, dude, I agree one hundred percent with you that it's crazy," Grady said. "But this particular book does communicate with your mind somehow."

Still without looking at her boyfriend, Molly grabbed Ricky by the thigh. "Quit doubting and try it. Read along with me."

Ricky stared hard at Grady. "You two ain't pulling my legs?"

Grady lowered his beer can from his lips. "I swear to God that we ain't."

"Okay then." With a look of dread on his face, Rick concentrated on the book too.

Grady finished up his can of beer.

"Hey, is it okay I get another from the kitchen?" he asked Ricky.

Ricky didn't reply. Ricky now also had that glazed look in his eyes and was staring down into the book with trembling lips. He'd begun breathing hard too.

Grady looked down and winced. Molly's grip on Ricky's left thigh had tightened, to the point where her fingernails were digging into his skin below the hem of his shorts. Molly's nails had begun drawing blood; red liquid beads welled up around her fingertips.

Because Molly was holding his leg now, Ricky had taken over the job of turning the pages.

Grady shivered. He tried going over to them both to break their concentration on what they were reading, but then found that he couldn't. He sensed a force there with them in the living room; a barrier that prevented him stepping towards his friends.

"Guys, concerning my request for another beer, I'll just assume silence means consent," Grady finally said. By now, the blood was running freely down Ricky's thigh and onto the couch.

The invisible barrier apparently only existed if Grady moved towards his friends. So instead, he walked quickly off into Ricky's kitchen and opened up his fridge.

CHAPTER 18

What the hell is going on? Grady wondered while getting out his next beer from Ricky's fridge. *Just like pops last night, Ricky and his new babe are spaced out on the book.*

Since yesterday, Grady had avoided looking at the little skin-bound book again. But for some reason (he couldn't have said how or why) he'd kept carrying the book around with him. Somehow, it would be in one of his pockets, though he'd not remember placing it in there.

Grady now felt that his sole glance into 'How to Succeed in Life' while in the company of his father and older sister—with that accompanying revelation of its title—seemed to have marked him in some way.

I feel like I'm destined to read 'How to Succeed in Life.' It's almost like the book wants me to read it. Like it's a curse hanging over me now!

When Grady returned to the living room with his beer, Ricky and Molly were still staring into the book. Grady's fresh attempt to walk in their direction was once more thwarted by that invisible resistance (which he now likened more to a mental revulsion that prevented progress than an actual physical barrier), and so he once more headed over to his armchair.

He watched Ricky turn to another page of the evil little volume.

How can I snap them out of it? Grady wondered while opening up his beer. *Do I call Ricky's cellphone or what?*

But then he saw that he'd already done it. The sharp hiss of air escaping from the beer can when he popped the tab snapped both Ricky and Molly out of their daze.

With horrified looks on their faces, both of them looked up from the book and stared at each other.

"That was just so wonderful," Molly said dreamily.

"And so horrible too," Ricky agreed in a perplexed voice. Then he howled in pain and looked down at his bloody left leg. "Fuck! What did you do to me!?"

Molly also looked down at his leg, and then she moaned in horror and pulled her hand off of his thigh.

"Oh, baby, I don't know what happened," she gasped at Ricky while examining her own bloody fingertips. "Do you have a first aid kit?"

Ricky didn't reply. Wincing in pain, he studied his thigh, turning it left and right. The blood on both his thigh and Molly's hand had already dried, and from where Grady sat, he could see three red semicircular indents amidst Ricky's thigh hair, from which, like the sources of rivers, several red lines had their origin.

"What happened? How did I do this to him?" Molly asked Grady helplessly.

"*You* didn't do it; the book did," Grady told her. "You two were staring into it for at least ten minutes."

When he said this, Ricky stopped examining his wounds and gave him a troubled look. "We were reading it for that long?" After asking this question, he looked first at Molly and then back at Grady. "Ten full minutes?"

Grady nodded. "What did you read inside it anyway? How does one succeed in life? I'm assuming this find of mine isn't your average self-help manual."

While Ricky continued looking troubled, Molly waved the book at Grady. "Well, it's a *satanic* self-help manual," she began saying. "What it says is that one needs to . . ." She frowned. "Yeah . . . what you're supposed to do is . . . you . . ." Molly stared at Grady in surprise. "Hey, I don't remember a thing of what I just read."

When Molly said this Grady had been about taking a sip of beer. But now he lowered the can. "What? You don't remember *anything?* As in, nothing at all?"

Looking confused now, Molly nodded and then turned to her boyfriend. "Sweetie, help me out here? Do you remember what we just read? Cuz I don't remember a thing of it."

Ricky nodded. "Yeah, the book says that you need to . . . that's right, to be successful in life is easy, one just needs to . . ." Ricky frowned at first, then he scowled and snatched the book from Molly. "Hey, what is this shit?" he asked, flipping angrily through its leather pages. Then he stared accusingly at Grady. "Dude, how come I can't remember any of the stuff inside it either?"

Grady recognized the look that Ricky now had on his face. Ricky was about at that point where he'd had enough of his confusion. Grady could almost read his best friend's mind: Ricky was about to fling the book on the gas range in the kitchen and then hit the igniter button.

Knowing what was coming if he didn't quickly intervene, Grady got to his feet and hurried over to the couch and snatched the book from Ricky's grasp.

In the meantime, Molly had left the living room.

"I don't know what to make of this," Grady told his best friend once the book was safely back inside his jacket, on the assumption that out of sight was out of mind too. "And right now, I'm really sorry that I took it away from the crime scene last night. I wish I could rewind that mistake now, but I'm sensing it's already too late. It's like taking the book away from there set something odd in motion, which I've got to figure out."

Ricky grunted back an indistinct reply, and then winced in pain and gripped his thigh. "Dammit, bro, I never thought girls' nails were so sharp."

Grady's mental question as to where Molly had vanished to were answered when she reappeared from the direction of the bedroom with a bowl of water and the first-aid kit from Ricky's bathroom.

She sat beside Ricky and began wiping the blood off of his thigh. She looked really upset. She was clearly sorry that she'd hurt Ricky.

"Doesn't look like you'll need any stitches," Grady told Ricky. "It don't look too bad."

Ricky winced as Molly rubbed antiseptic salve onto the three angry red indents. "Easy for you to say, dude. Leg feels like shit."

"You should be grateful I didn't accidentally grab your dick," Molly told Ricky testily.

"Ouch!" Grady said and resumed drinking his beer.

"Sweetie, it was the book's fault not mine," Molly told Ricky apologetically on seeing the angry look on his face after her 'dick' comment. "Honest, I'd never do anything nasty like this intentionally."

"Dude, just get the book out of my house," Ricky told Grady. "Keep that thing well away from me and Molly." He leaned over and kissed her. "I may not remember what I read in that creepy little book, but I recall it was really horrible, all completely nasty stuff."

He looked at Molly, who nodded back at him.

"Yeah, it was nasty stuff," she agreed, clearly desperate to not anger Ricky again. But her eyes told Grady a different story. Molly looked as if she remembered something nice amidst all of the horrors that she'd read.

CHAPTER 19

The passage of time dulls even the strongest of impressions.

By nighttime, Gina already found yesterday's 'phone call of the dead' hazy and unreal. Not unreal in the sense of it having been an unreal experience, but in the sense of it 'might not have really happened at all.'

Yeah, a whole shift of handling pizza orders will do that to you, she thought.

She was in Susan's bedroom, toweling her hair dry after having a shower, and getting ready for bed.

She smiled when Susan pressed up against her back and kissed her neck. She was naked and Susan was nude too. Susan's huge body felt warm and soft, like she was the dough she made pizzas from.

"Ooh yes, baby," Gina gasped.

She relaxed back against the older woman, feeling like she was sinking into her flesh, feeling Susan's nipples stiffen against her back.

Yes, like Gina had earlier told Grady, she didn't love Susan Bundy and was only with the older woman for the financial benefits that their relationship brought her. But Gina *loved* the way Susan's big body felt. Gina loved the sensation of having so much *person* wrapped around her. Sometimes when making love with Susan, Gina felt she was making love to more than one person at once.

Susan wrapped her arms around her. While Gina finished toweling off her hair, Susan turned her around so that they were face-to-face and then kissed her. Gina had to tilt her head upwards to reach her tongue and lips; Susan was taller than she was.

They kissed for a while, and Gina felt most of the day's stress slip away from her. In sync with her emotions, she let the towel in her hands slip to the floor and wrapped her arms around her lover's neck while their tongues tangled like mating snakes.

"Hey, what's this you're holding?" Gina asked Susan after they'd separated.

Susan lifted the book in her hand. "Oh, you mean this? I dunno what it is."

Her reply confused Gina. "What do you mean, you don't know? It's a book, isn't it?"

Susan handed the book over to Gina. "Here, you look at it and you'll understand what I mean."

Gina held the book up. It was small, cellphone-sized but not much thicker than one of the pizzeria's menus. Strangely it seemed made of skin, tanned to leather, of course.

Then Gina understood what her girlfriend meant: "What kinda crappy writing is this?" she asked in puzzlement.

"See what I mean, darling?" Susan replied with a gesture at the strange book in Gina's hands. "I've no frigging idea what's written on its cover." But then, she shook her head. "No, no—that's wrong. Somehow I know it's called 'How to Succeed in Life.' "

Gina frowned at her. "How can you know that?"

Susan shrugged. "I dunno, but I know that's what it says."

Gina flipped through the pages, which were filled with similar red-and-brown-letter gobbledygook. "So, how'd you get it anyway?"

Susan backed off from her and sat on the edge of the bed. "Well, according to Katie, this weird guy came in to buy a pizza this afternoon and he forgot it."

Gina gave her an inquiring look that requested further info. Katie had worked the evening/night shift at the shop counter.

Susan shrugged. "That's it. He came in, bought his pizza, and left with it. Then after he'd gone, Katie saw the book on the counter and figured it was his. She expected him to come back for it, but he didn't. When I came out of the kitchen for a breather, she showed the book to me. It's been with me ever since." Susan's normally pleasant plump face now grew a worried expression. "I dunno why I keep carrying it around, but I do. I've never seen anything like that language before, but once I look at it, I feel that if I think hard enough, I'll be able to get the meaning of the words; just like I somehow got what the cover means."

Gina laughed uneasily, as the shadow of last night's impossible conversation with a corpse threatened to return and haunt her again. Somehow, this felt just as creepy; particularly because, now that she'd been holding the book for a while, its texture felt unnatural for dead leather; rather it felt as warm as if it was the skin of a living human hand she was clasping.

"Well, let's forget the book for a while," she told Susan, dropping it on top of the dresser. Then she moved over to the bed and pushed Susan down flat on it.

"Make love to me, baby," she whispered in Susan's ear after kissing her lips again. "The damn book will still be here tomorrow."

Susan began making love to her. Gina began moaning gently. She knew this wouldn't be over until the fat woman came.

"You do love me, don't you, honey?" Susan asked gently afterwards, holding Gina's hand in hers as they lay side by side.

Gina had been expecting this question. They had this afterglow conversation on a regular basis.

"Of course, I love you," she lied, turning to Susan and smiling at her.

Susan moved closer to her, so that their bodies were touching again.

"I mean it, you do really love me, don't you?" she went on, her voice now taking on the whiny nasal tone that Gina dreaded and hated. "You're not just with me because I treat you well and buy you lots of gifts and clothes?"

Gina sighed deeply. "Honey, I don't know why you keep on asking me this," she replied. She patted Susan's giant belly. "Of course, I love you. You're my whole world." She kissed Susan. "Now let's go to sleep," she said sweetly after the kiss.

Satisfied by Gina's lies, Susan quickly fell asleep.

Gina remained awake, however.

I really need to break up with Susan, she thought. *Soon she's gonna start suggesting that if I love her as much as I claim to, we should get married. What do I do? Susan's brother likes me too—I catch Joe staring at me when he thinks I'm too busy to notice. But it's sleazy to drop the sister and date the brother instead, but maybe—*

While thinking in this manner, Gina's gaze had been roving around the bedroom. And right now, her eyes found the weird book she'd earlier dropped on the dresser.

Unable to fall asleep, she got out of bed and crossed over to the dresser.

I'll just see if Susan was telling the truth about being able to read this thing even without understanding it, Gina thought as she picked up the strange little book.

CHAPTER 20

"You still going to the beach with Ricky and his new girlfriend?" Kayla asked Grady at breakfast on Saturday morning.

"Uh huh," he mouthed around a mouthful of toast.

Their father Tommy gave them both a searching look over his mug of coffee and then returned to checking out the financial news on his cellphone.

Grady had today off, and so also did both Ricky and Molly. The three of them had thus planned a trip over to the seafront town of Plymouth for that Saturday afternoon.

"Maybe I'll come to the beach with you three," Kayla said.

Tommy Burke looked at his daughter in surprise. "Why?" he asked in a worried voice. "Are you thinking of filming a solo porn scene by the sea? Please don't, hon. You can get arrested for indecent exposure."

She shook her head. "Nothing of the sort, pops. I'm trying to balance Grady's equation. I'm concerned about his love life. Pops, the last time Grady had a date was six months ago."

"Maybe that's for the best," Tommy Burke told her. "You, honey, do enough *dating* for all three of us. Actually you do enough *dating* for our entire street."

"I think I'm currently asexual," Grady opined. "I don't even watch porn anymore."

Kayla went on speaking as if neither of the others had spoken.

"You need to find yourself a girlfriend," she told Grady. "When you're out by the sea today, you're gonna be in the way, cock-blocking Ricky when he wants a blowjob on the summer sand."

Grady said, "Look who's talking. Sis, do you have a boyfriend?"

Kayla smiled coyly back at him. "I don't need one. I'm having my emotional and physical needs met anyway."

"And worldwide on live television for that matter," Grady said, and then ducked when Kayla flicked the slice of bacon on her fork at him.

"Hey, hey, cut it out, both of ya!" their father told them. "It's bad enough neither of you having a relationship with someone, but don't get bacon in my coffee cuz of it."

"Sorry, pops," Grady apologized.

Kayla said: "Hey, pops, what I'm saying is: if I go to the beach with Grady and Ricky, folks will naturally assume I'm his girlfriend. Then, because I'm hot, all of the similarly hot chicks at the beach will contest for his attention, and he'll get lots of phone numbers and . . ." She giggled disarmingly at their father. "Nah, pops, I really just wanna work on my tan."

Grady sighed and said, "Yeah, yeah, come along, just don't pack your Vaseline." Then he turned to their dad. "Pops, that's a good point tho—none of the three of us has anyone we're seeing regularly. Pops, don't you get lonely sometimes?"

Tommy Burke lowered his coffee mug and gave them both an embarrassed smile. "C'mon, you guys, don't tease an old man. You know what happened the last time I went out with a woman." His smile turned grim. "You guys can't imagine what it was like—waking up in that motel with my wallet and money gone. I'm surprised she didn't steal my phone too."

"Dad, calm down," Kayla said.

"I felt like the world's greatest fool," Tommy Burke said. "It was as bad as I'm sure an acrimonious divorce must be; to be taken for all you have by some damn scheming broad." Grady noticed that his father had unconsciously shaped his hands and fingers as if he was strangling someone with them, and the expression on his face was a distant one; he didn't seem to be in the dining room with them anymore. "But I'm certain that one of these days, I'm gonna come face-to-face with that pretty identity thief and then I'm gonna . . . I'm gonna . . . I'm . . ."

"Pops, snap out of it!" Kayla said sharply, jabbing the tines of her fork, bacon and all, into her father's tightened fingers.

Tommy Burke's eyes slowly regained focus. "I'm sorry, kids. I can't help losing it each time I recall that bitch Anita. It's a good thing I've not found her yet—If I had you two might be visiting me behind bars now."

"You're taking this thing too seriously," Kayla said. "Just because one woman stole your money doesn't mean all of them will."

Tommy looked like he'd disagree with Kayla but then nodded. "Yep, guess you're right, sweetie. I'd better get over it."

"Yes, you should, pops," Kayla agreed with a sweet smile.

Grady nodded. "And the sooner the better. And besides, that bitch who robbed you like that was an *escort*; I'm talking of dating a regular woman . . . someone like Mrs. Smith next door. It's clear as broad daylight that she likes you."

"Yeah, that's true," Kayla said, spearing another slice of bacon. "Annie is lonely; she needs a man. I see her make love-me eyes at you on a regular basis. Don't lie that you haven't noticed that too."

Tommy Burke nodded. "Yeah, yeah, I have. I've thought 'bout dating Annie more than once. But nah, those kids of hers are just too bratty for comfort."

"Hey, or I could set you up with someone," Kayla added. "Lots of the women who come here to see me like you. They've told me so."

Both Grady and his father looked at her.

Finally Tommy Burke rolled his eyes. "Honey, you forget that all of your girlfriends have dicks like you."

Kayla nodded. "Oh, I'd only introduce you to bottoms. You won't notice the difference. I promise, pops. And it's tighter back there too."

Grady smiled at his father. "Looks like you're caught between a rock and a hard cock, pops. I wonder which you'll choose?"

Tom Burke rolled his eyes again. "Son, if those are my alternatives, I'd rather become asexual like you."

CHAPTER 21

Unknown to his two grownup children, Tommy Burke had been having a hard time for the past two days. He found that he kept reading the horrible little book that he'd mysteriously 'downloaded.'

Each time Tommy read the book, he quickly grew disgusted with its contents and flung it across the room. But after a while he'd feel a compulsion to pick it up and start reading it again.

Tommy still never remembered what he'd read inside the book, all he knew was that each time he dropped it, he felt like vomiting.

Tommy Burke also knew that the reason he never remembered what he'd read afterwards was because he'd not yet read far enough into 'How to Succeed in Life.'

There was an unwritten law in effect here: the book's contents had a 'point of no return,' a point beyond which the non-acceptance of its offer was no longer an option.

Tommy suspected that once he reached that critical point, he would have to do what the book demanded of him or face the consequences.

But I don't wanna do any of that crap! I wish I could just remember what it was. I'm not doing it and that's that!

But Tommy had discovered that each time he picked the book up and continued reading through it, he read further into it than he had the previous time. Meaning, his 'point of no return' would soon be reached.

When I'll likely have a full understanding of both my fantastic success and my accompanying damnation.

Being a good and loving father, Tommy didn't want to involve Grady and Kayla in the mess he'd found himself. Both of his children seemed okay, so far untouched by the madness that he felt spiraling around him.

With no way out of his problem, Tommy was drinking to calm himself. The downside of doing this was that the more Tommy drunk, the more he lost his self-control and the more susceptible to the book's demand to be read he became.

But the positive side of getting drunk (and remaining in that state) which Tommy Burke had quickly discovered, was that, when he was drunk, he couldn't understand the book. He'd pick it up, stare at the pages for hours and not understand a thing.

Tommy sensed the book's frustration with this. And so, he kept right on drinking.

It was an uneasy stalemate. But for the moment at least, Tommy Burke was in a safe place.

CHAPTER 22

"Yeah, you guys had better come in the house and wait," Grady told Ricky on the phone. "Kayla's insisting that she wants to come to the beach with us and I don't know if she's ready to go yet."

That said, Grady dropped his cellphone on his bed and left his room to go let in his friends.

Stepping out into the upper hallway, Grady felt a moment's apprehension.

He was used to encountering strange people upstairs in their house. He sometimes felt that he was living in a dormitory of Unisex, the college where Kayla, as dean, taught shemale fucking.

The folks he encountered upstairs were often partially naked, or in the case of Mr. and Mrs. Stainless Strange (a strange name if he'd ever heard one) they were completely covered in colored latex but always had throbbing erections jutting out of their crotches. Disconcerting to say the least.

I suppose the Stainless Stranges let their penises out for air once they step onto the stairs here—no way can they have driven over in their car with their dicks sticking out like that.

Thankfully, today wasn't one of those days when strange people with strange sexual fetishes lingered in the upstairs hallway like partygoers needing to use the bathroom.

Grady walked down the hallway. Kayla had the front bedroom. Grady paused by her door and knocked.

"Hey, sis! Ricky and Molly are here!" he called out.

"Alright, gimme a few minutes!" she called back. "I'm putting on my makeup!"

"Shake a leg!"

Grady left Kayla's door and walked to the stairs. While descending to the living room, his mind once more rolled over his earlier insight concerning his family:

Yep, none of the three of us are in any meaningful relationship. I, at the ripe old age of twenty-three, appear to have lost interest in the opposite sex, or in any sex at all for that matter. My dad is angry with women because of a hooker who screwed him over. And last but most definitely not least, my older sister is a confirmed slut; a shemale slut of steadily growing international repute.

Downstairs, his father Tommy was watching a tennis match on the TV. Grady was surprised to see his pops drinking so early in the day and drinking so much too. Tommy had a half-empty bottle of Wild Turkey by his elbow, and if Grady's memory served him correctly, yesterday that same bottle of bourbon whiskey had been unopened.

A quick glance over at the liquor cabinet confirmed that, yes, it was the same bottle of whiskey.

"Hey, pops, you okay?" Grady asked.

Tommy turned to look at him. "Huh, son?"

"I'm just wondering why you're drinking so early in the day. That's so unlike you."

Tommy nodded. "Yeah, son. But . . . I got some stuff on my mind. I need to relax a little."

Grady was about to say more, when the front doorbell rang.

Tommy now looked bothered. "That ain't some more of Kayla's porno clique, is it? I thought she was gonna go the beach with you."

"It's okay, pops, that should be Ricky."

The doorbell rang again. Grady left his father to go and let Ricky in.

"Hey, man," Ricky told him once he'd opened the front door. "Kayla ready yet?"

"Still putting on her favorite face." Grady then smiled at Molly. "Hey there." Then he stepped back. "You guys had better come in and wait." Then Grady lowered his voice to a whisper and after a glance back, added: "Hey, don't talk too loud. I dunno what's up with pops today. He's drinking like he's trying to drown himself."

"Maybe we should wait in the car then," Molly suggested.

Grady shook his head. "Nah, come on in. We'll go up to my room and listen to music."

Ricky and Molly stepped inside and Grady shut the door behind them.

"Hi, Mr. Burke!" Ricky called out as they walked towards the stairs.

Tommy turned from staring at the mixed doubles match on the television. His face lit up with a smile of drunken recognition.

"Hey, son, how you do—"

Tommy had been waving at Ricky but then froze when he spotted Molly.

"W-we-well, I'll be d-damned!" Tommy sputtered suddenly. "If it ain't th-the d-d-devil herself!"

His comment surprised Grady. And Grady became even more surprised when he saw that Molly had begun trembling. She was staring at Tommy Burke in horror, like she recognized him from one of her nightmares.

"Anita, you damn thieving slut!" Tommy growled and launched himself out of his chair. "I knew I'd find you someday!"

Ricky was staring at Grady in confusion. Then both young men stared at Molly instead.

Molly had already let go of Ricky, turned around, and was running for the front door.

But she'd left her flight too late. Even drunk as he was, Tommy Burke came after her like a freight train.

He grabbed Molly before she was even halfway to his front door and spun her around to face him.

"Yeah, it is you!" he yelled in her surprised and scared face. "Damn thieving prostitute bitch! What the hell did you do with my wallet!?"

"Pops, what going on?" Grady asked weakly.

"She's the goddamned hooker I told you boys about!" Tommy growled back at him. "The one who stole my wallet two months ago!"

Grady stared at Ricky, who was staring back at him with crazy questions in his eyes. Ricky knew the story of Tommy's mishap with an escort. The story had been a hilarious joke back then. But his own girlfriend?

"Hey, old man, you're mistaking me for someone else," Molly protested weakly. But her voice lacked any conviction. It was obvious she was lying.

Tommy was almost foaming at the mouth now.

"Hey, let go of me! You're hurting me!" Molly said.

Instead of letting her go, Tommy shook her violently. "I knew it was you, Anita. Damn whore. Hey, where is my wallet, you damn puta?"

"You're a hooker?" Ricky asked Molly.

"Was, was, was!" Molly almost wept back. "It happened for a bit after my aunt fired me. I was about to lose my apartment, so I decided to do some sex work."

Her voice was coming out all wobbly because Tommy was shaking her like she was a rag doll.

"Girl, where is my damn wallet and my credit cards and my money?" he demanded.

"Let go of me, old man. I don't have them. I never stole your stuff!"

"Liar!"

"Let go of me. You're hurting me."

Then Tommy slapped Molly. "Liar! Where is my wallet?"

On being hit, a change came over Molly. From being scared and on the defense, her eyes flared up in rage and she practically lunged at Tommy Burke.

And then she spat in Tommy's face.

"Hey, what's all the commotion down there?" Kayla called from upstairs.

No one replied her. Both Grady and Ricky seemed rooted in place, too startled to prevent what was happening in front of them.

Tommy still had a firm hold of Molly with his left hand. Molly, however, was no longer making any attempt to get away from him. Her eyes dared him to do his worst.

"You dare spit on me?" Tommy asked, wiped the spittle from his face.

He slapped Molly twice more in rapid succession, this time splitting her upper lip.

Once more, Molly didn't back down. Instead, with blood now dribbling from her split lip, she spat in Tommy Burke's face again.

"Yes, so I got your damn wallet and your money, old man!" she screamed at him. "I spent your damn money on shoes." She began kicking him. "I bought these shoes I'm wearing with your money!" She spat again at Tommy's face again, but this time he ducked and she missed. "How dare you hit me? Fuck you! Fuck you!"

The look on Tommy's elderly face now was like he'd kill Molly, so help him God.

Seeing that incensed look unfroze Grady and Ricky and they quickly separated the dueling pair. Ricky pulled Molly backward while Grady prized his father's fingers off of Molly's arm.

"Damn hookers can't never be trusted," Tommy grumbled as Grady forced him back towards his chair.

"Hey, what's all the fuss?" Kayla asked, now descending the stairs. Kayla had a broad-brimmed straw hat on her head and a rainbow-colored beach bag slung over her shoulder. Her pink tee shirt read: 'ONE MAN'S ASS IS ANOTHER MAN'S PUSSY.'

Kayla gasped when she saw Molly dabbing blood from her lip with a handkerchief. "Everyone, what's going on down here!?"

"It's alright now," Grady replied her. "Pops just discovered that Molly is the escort who stole his wallet."

"For real?" On hearing this, Kayla hurried down the stairs, dropped her beach bag on the floor, and walked over to stare at Molly. "You're the one who stole my daddy's wallet?"

Molly shrugged defiantly back at her.

"Well, looks like my daddy has slapped his stolen three hundred buck's worth out of you," Kayla said coolly. "Hopefully we can all be friends now."

All this while, Ricky had been looking perplexed. He was still holding fast onto Molly, who was pulling against his restraint as if she wanted to go spit on Tommy some more.

"You okay, pops?" Kayla asked her father, who was pouring himself a fresh drink of whiskey.

"Yeah, yeah, I'm fine now," Tommy said. "Seeing that thieving bitch over there"—he made a dismissive gesture in Molly's direction—"I just completely lost it for a few seconds."

Still fighting against Ricky's restraint, Molly stared at Tommy with hatred in her eyes. "Listen, old man," she spat at him, "Yes, I still have your damn wallet. And you know what? My aunt Melda is a witch, and I'm gonna give your wallet and ID to her and have her curse you and cause you to die a very painful death for making me bleed like this."

"Geez, give it a rest already," Kayla told her a little angrily.

Tommy sipped his whiskey and laughed at Molly's threat. "Oh, fuck off, you thieving slut, before I come over there and give you some more of what you deserve. Like Kayla said, I ain't abusing you any, I just gave you the beating you paid for." Then he frowned, and gave Molly a disgusted look. "With all of the dirty dicks you've been sucking, I just hope I don't catch an STD from all of that spitting on me that you just did."

His words merely incensed Molly the more. "You're gonna die from my aunt's curse, old man!"

"Girl, get the hell outa my house before I come throw you out!" was Tommy's response to this.

"Hahaha!" Molly taunted him with a cold smile on her face, and with Ricky still holding her in place. "Your death is gonna be excruciatingly painful! Your guts are gonna explode like bombs. How dare you hit me and make me bleed like this!"

"I think you need another dose of hitting," Tommy said, getting to his feet. "Let's just say this additional beating is the interest you owe on that money you stole."

Grady quickly blocked his father off from crossing the living room.

"Oh no, pops, you just sit back down now," he told Tommy Burke as he forced him back down on the armchair. "We don't need any more violence out of you."

"Get Molly out of here," Kayla told Ricky. "You two go wait outside in the car for us."

"Come on, let's go wait in my car," Ricky told Molly.

Molly stared at him in contempt. "Why?"

"Because, you're mostly in the wrong here," Ricky said. "What the heck did you go and steal his wallet for?"

When Molly still refused to budge from that spot, Ricky shrugged and then forcibly picked her up.

Molly might have had large breasts, but the rest of her was quite small, and so Ricky easily placed her over his shoulder and bore her off to the front door and out of the house.

Molly went uncomplaining, like she was surprised she was that easy to pick up and carry away.

Tommy laughed as the door shut on the pair. "Ricky had better get his money's worth out of that slut's ass while it's still free . . . before she takes him to the cleaners," he said.

"Okay, pops, are you gonna be okay if we leave you at home?" Kayla asked her father.

Tommy nodded and laughed. "Yeah, I ain't angry any longer. Now I've got closure on the incident." Then he scowled at Kayla. "Listen, girl, now that you know that Ricky's girlfriend is a prostitute, I draw the line at her coming here to film porn with you. We can't both be banging the same women."

Kayla looked amused. "Pops, but I'd . . . I'd never . . . I-I . . ."

Tommy kept on frowning at her. "I've heard that one before, honey."

Kayla sighed and turned to Grady. "So, can we go to the beach now?"

Grady nodded. "I guess so, so long as Ricky and Molly don't break up during the journey to Plymouth."

Kayla picked up her rainbow beach bag again. "Yeah, finding out that your new babe used to be a sex worker can really throw a monkey wrench in the gears of romance."

CHAPTER 23

The drive out to Plymouth was a weird one. This was entirely because Ricky, who should have driven his car, spent the entirely of the trip in the backseat consoling Molly, who spent the entire trip crying.

Grady hadn't brought along his driver's license, so Kayla, who had hers in her purse, drove the blue Hyundai.

"Tears are a great cover up for a woman," Kayla told Grady when they stopped to buy gasoline and both got out of the car. "Now instead of Ricky being pissed off with Molly cuz of her questionable morals, now *he* has to comfort *her* all through the trip. Real or faked, a woman's crying always appeals to the protective part of a man's nature. Tears also make us ladies seem we're in the right when we're clearly in the wrong."

They made the beach in good time. As the weather prophets had foretold, the afternoon was gloriously sunny, with the only rain in sight that coming from Molly's eyes.

"I can no longer tell if her face is puffy from her being slapped or from crying so much," Ricky complained to Grady and Kayla out of Molly's hearing.

Grady had been staring out at the ocean, which shimmered in entrancing blue ripples. Now he glanced over at Molly, who lay on her back on a beach towel. The glance served to confirm what he'd agreed on before: Molly's bikini top was five or six sizes too small.

Kayla smiled sympathetically at Ricky, then gestured over at his miserable girlfriend. "She just needs more comforting. She's really upset. Hey, but do you even still want her?"

Ricky nodded. "Yeah, it's okay. The past is past. Would've been better if she'd told me herself tho'. Imagine if the guy she'd stolen from had been some random fellow we ran into in the grocery shop."

Kayla laid a hand on Ricky's shoulder. "Well, since you're not about dumping her for her past sexual behavior, there's only one thing for it."

"What's that?" Ricky asked. "I'll do anything to stop her crying. Else, she's gonna ruin this trip for all of us."

Kayla looked around the beach. "Well, we're the only ones on this stretch of beach, so you'll be fine if you fuck her here."

Ricky looked askance at Kayla, then asked, "Fuck Molly . . . here . . . ?"

Kayla gestured out at the ocean blue, then stared up at the clouds with their freckling of seagulls. "Women find public sex stimulating . . . you know. Don't worry, you'll be completely alone. Grady and I will go wait in the car till you're done. We'll phone you if anyone appears to disrupt your private party."

Ricky looked dubiously back at Molly. At the moment Molly was wiping tears from her eyes.

"You sure she's gonna want to?" he asked Kayla. "I mean . . . out here in public?"

"Oh, it's okay, there's enough tree cover here to prevent you being noticed from higher up the shore." Kayla laughed and grabbed the crotch of Ricky's swim trunks. "Go give her some of this. You'll be surprised at the results."

Ricky shrugged. "Okay, I'll go do it."

Kayla watched him walk back to Molly, and then she crooked a finger at Grady. "C'mon, little brother, let's go wait till they've come."

Grady followed her up the slope of the beach until they were out of sight of their friends.

"Kayla, you sure that will work?"

Kayla smiled sweetly. "Trust me, the little slut is just putting on a show for Ricky. Her crocodile tears will dry up the moment he gets his dick out."

CHAPTER 24

They sat in the car listening to the radio. Out on the highway, a few cars passed by, but none turned in toward the beach.

The sun was nice and warm. But here in the car, even with the doors open, it was hot, and Grady had begun sweating in his swim trunks. Feeling the heat liquefy out of the pores of his cloth-constrained crotch, he wished he were swimming out in the cool and deep blue.

His sister, though, seemed cool as ice cream. Kayla wasn't breaking a sweat in her green bikini. But then, that was Kayla: pretty as the proverbial picture and as unruffled as the clouds in today's sky.

"Want a beer?" Kayla asked all of a sudden.

"Yeah, sure."

Kayla turned back between the seats and began fishing in the spare drinks cooler in the rear footwell.

"Hey, why'd you bring this along?" she asked all of a sudden.

Grady had been nodding his head to Slain Jane on the radio, but now he turned to Kayla. "Huh? Bring what?"

"Hold on and I'll show you."

When Kayla pulled herself back into the front half of the car, she was holding two cans of beer and the book 'How to Succeed in Life.'

"Where the hell did that come from?" Grady asked.

"It was sticking out from your pants pocket. Why did you bring it here?"

Grady shook his head at her. "I didn't. I dunno how it got here." He saw that she didn't believe him. "Listen, sis, the last time I saw that book was when I dropped it in the bottom drawer of the nightstand beside my bed yesterday."

Kayla frowned. "And now it's here at the beach with us. You know, maybe the book is female and it's following you around cuz you don't have a girlfriend yet."

"Somehow, that is both believable and unfunny." Grady took his beer from her, and then accepted the book also from her fingers.

With unpleasant thoughts swirling in his head, he drank his beer.

"Have you figured out the rest of what it says?" Kayla asked him after they'd been drinking for a while.

Grady shook his head at her. "Uh uh. I'm afraid to even read it. And I'm just as afraid to throw it away." He flapped his right hand upward at the sun. "You know, in case I get back home after doing so, and there it is waiting for me again at home."

Kayla laughed. "Soon you'll be expecting me to believe in ghosts."

Grady laughed too. Staring at the creepy book, he felt a sudden pull to open it up and read its contents. But he steeled himself against doing so.

Correctly interpreting the conflicted look on her brother's face, Kayla became very amused. "You might as well read it to pass the time while we're waiting here in the car," she advised him. "If Molly needs as much comforting as I think she does, we'll be here for up to an hour. Possibly more."

Grady rolled his eyes. "Seriously? I mean Molly, not the book."

"I mean it," Kayla went on. "First of all, Molly is certain to need oral comforting; sad women generally do—cunnilingus helps us replenish lost water and by now Molly has lost liters of water as tears. Then Molly will definitely need vaginal comforting." Kayla sighed. "And then, if Ricky's up to it, she might even need anal comforting."

Grady burst out laughing. "Sis, you are so filthy-minded, I'm ashamed to be related to you."

Kayla shrugged back at him. "Wait and see, once we get back to the beach, it'll be as if Molly never suffered any humiliation or wept a single tear today. And . . . get this: if Molly is the kind of committed young woman that I suspect she is—she'll do everything in her power to keep Ricky, who after all is quite the hunk. I assure you, to show Ricky how much she loves him, Molly may even need a golden shower to wash her soiled emotions clean again."

"Okay, if you say so."

"Hey, forget those two," Kayla said. "While they're making up, you can help me out with something." She jerked her thumb back between the seats. "Listen, finish off your beer and put that silly book away in your pocket again. And when you're done with that, come film me." Now, Kayla gestured at the lush green landscape outside of the car. "I'm long overdue to post some photos and videos on my xHamster page."

"Okay," Grady agreed. "But no dick pics."

But his sister was already popping her penis out of her bikini bottom. "C'mon, Grady, I gotta give my fans what they want."

Grady's eyes popped wide open. "Sis, NO!"

"What are you so worried about? There's no one here except us. Besides, it's not like I'm asking *you* to suck me off."

Grady sighed. Then he put the book back into his pants pocket and began filming Kayla.

Grady filmed Kayla. And from such innocuous beginning as her just having her penis out, her solo sex session turned very gross indeed.

CHAPTER 25

When Ricky called and gave them the all-clear an hour later, Grady found out that Kayla been right; Molly was a completely rejuvenated young woman. Gone were all of her tears. Now she was fun and games again.

Grady was surprised at how accurate his sister's prediction had been. When he stood close to Molly before she ran off into the ocean to swim, she smelled of piss, like she'd somehow gotten some on her face. And her skimpy bikini top was completely soaked through, even though she'd not yet been in the water.

Grady grinned to himself. Molly clearly hadn't *wept* that much.

CHAPTER 26

I don't get it, Tommy Burke thought to himself late that night. *Why the hell did I react that violently on meeting that girl? That was completely unlike me. Yeah, I know I was angry at her stealing my ID like that, but it's been several months now, and aside from my reduced interest in hiring hookers and escorts, I've been over her betrayal for ages. But the moment I saw her—Anita . . . Molly . . . whatever—a crazy rage built up inside of me, like I wanted to kill her.*

Tommy frowned as an additional memory came to his mind:

And the mean way I was talking to her; like I beat up women for fun all the time! That's totally not me! That wasn't me at all!

Prior to that morning's incident, Tommy Burke had never hit a woman in his life. Violence against women was as alien to his nature as taking a crap in a public place was.

Unable to sleep tonight, Tommy had been sitting at his work desk for the past hour.

Marko Velli needed to liquefy some funds—something about a house here in Raynham that he wanted to buy for his mother, though Tommy wasn't privy to all of the details.

Tommy had decided to get on it tonight. So, after fetching himself a bottle of wine from the bar in his living room, he'd sat down to figure out exactly which of the mob kingpin's offshore accounts would be best to tap the required funds from, and then which onshore accounts to transfer the money to.

Tonight had been all stop-start. Tommy would work for a quarter-hour or so, and then the memories of the morning's reacquaintance with Anita/Molly would disrupt the golden flow of crypto and Tommy would take a break, pour himself more wine from the half-empty bottle of red on his work desk, and then ponder his uncharacteristic violent behavior.

And I really meant what I said then, about beating her up some more as interest! I mean, what the heck!?

Tommy shrugged off his puzzlement over his uncharacteristic behavior and returned to work. Marko's encoded money flowed in untraceable golden streams from faraway shores to the Land of the Free and the Home of the Brave.

Tommy drank a toast to his personal genius. *Come daylight, Marko Velli will be a very happy man indeed. One new house coming up!*

After a while, Tommy Burke took another break. Staring at his laptop, he wondered why *he* was the one doing this job for the Boston mob.

I thought the mob had accountants for stuff like this? That guy Johnny Horowitz; ain't this what Marko pays him for? Though Horowitz reputedly spends most of his time chasing pussy.

Tommy paused for a few moments and refilled his wineglass.

And now, with his attention temporarily off of both work and male-on-female violence, his unease about the creepy book in his possession returned.

All of a sudden, Tommy realized that the book 'How to Succeed in Life' was once more on his work desk. In fact, it was right by his left hand.

Alarm instantly flooded him and a feeling of cold horror poured over him. He jerked his hand away from the evil book, but, conscious of his son and daughter upstairs, managed not to scream out his fright.

The last thing I want to do now is wake up Kayla, who is certain to freak out.

But like a rabbit entranced by a snake, Tommy couldn't stop staring at the book and trembling in fright. He drank to calm himself, but his wineglass shook in his fingers and he spilled half of its contents on his laptop.

Dammit! I'm sure I left it in the bookcase, under those documents. I know I did!

Be that as it had been, 'How to Succeed in Life' now lay on Tommy's desk again. And, impossible though it was, crazy as it seemed even to himself, he could hear the nasty little book communicate its desires to him; not in words, but as an unmistakable sequence of wants and feelings.

Tommy sensed the book's expectance: its interest in being read and its need for him to accept what it offered, believe in its promises and in its ability to fulfil them, and then take specific horrible actions to get what he wanted.

He shook his head at it, and poured himself a full glass of wine. By now he'd gotten over his initial shock and his fingers didn't shake while he refilled the wineglass. Still, he gulped the red liquid down like it was water in the desert and then addressed the book on his desk:

"Sorry, book, but I ain't falling for it." he said aloud in a mock-theatrical voice. "I ain't reading ya, and that's that. Book, I don't want any of what you're selling. Just in case you haven't noticed"—and here Tommy gestured at the banking apps and financial spreadsheets opened up on his laptop—"I'm already an extremely successful man." Then Tommy sighed. "Yep, and I'm also holding conversations with a damn haunted book."

Earlier in the day, after Grady and Kayla had left for the beach, Tommy had realized that he didn't really need to be drunk to cope with the book. All he needed was to stay a little buzzed-up on alcohol. That was sufficient to dull any comprehension of the book's arcane text.

My liver won't like all of this drinking I'm doin' tho'.

Of course, the book didn't like his drinking either. Tommy knew it didn't. But Tommy didn't give a shit about what the book liked or disliked.

He did sense, however, that the book was now frustrated and annoyed with him.

He also sensed that the book was very dangerous. He just had no idea how dangerous it was.

CHAPTER 27

Seeing no point in going to the trouble to conceal the book from view only to have it turn up again on his desk, Tommy instead shoved the leather copy of 'How to Succeed in Life' out of sight behind his laptop.

Out of sight—hopefully out of mind too!

When he paid attention to his laptop again, a solitary email notification had just popped up in the notifications tab.

Tommy sighed on seeing it: 'fap2kayla69 just posted her beachfront photoshoot.'

Tommy frowned. *Yeah, I knew my li'l girl wasn't just going sunbathing.*

He still felt too frazzled from contact with the evil little book to return to work. And besides, most of tonight's work was finished anyway.

And yet, even with most of the bottle of wine gone, Tommy did not feel like going to bed.

So, to distract himself, Tommy Burke clicked on the email notification for his daughter's post.

The email contained a link and when he clicked on that it took him to Kayla's OnlyFans page.

O.K., now this is extremely ill-advised, Tommy told himself as he entered his email address and OnlyFans password. (As if Kayla wanted her family to appreciate how perverse she could be, she'd given free lifelong subscriptions to all of her exclusive content to both her father and her younger brother.)

I'm practically guaranteed to see something on her page that'll offend me.

His lips twisted up in a grimace when he remembered the first time (which was also the last time before tonight) that his curiosity had gotten the better of him and he'd investigated exactly what his transgender daughter was doing in sex-land.

The images of Kayla stuffing a massive cucumber up her ass while some masked transwoman masturbated her into a wineglass had made Tommy regret his curiosity. He was well aware that what he'd witnessed would be considered tame when compared to modern standards of porno degradation, but the fact that this was his own daughter . . . and a daughter who looked exactly like her late mother, had traumatized him for days afterwards.

Tommy had sworn never to visit any of Kayla's sex websites again. Afterwards, he'd wondered why the hell he'd checked out her OnlyFans in the first place.

You already knew that wasn't Instagram or TikTok or Facebook or YouTube.

And just like back then, right now Tommy wondered what the hell he was doing entering his password and clicking into Kayla's OnlyFans again—something he'd sworn he'd never do.

But all of a sudden, here he was, staring at her sitting on a beach towel spread over the hood of a blue Hyundai—*Yeah, that's Ricky's car*—with her penis out.

Tommy winced at the sight of the penis, which was already growing hard as Kayla stroked herself while addressing the camera:

"Okay, fans, this is your favorite transgirl fap2kayla69 with an impromptu shoot. Just a solo, today. No blowjobs cuz today it's my brother Grady handling the camera, and as far as I can remember, Grady ain't ever sucked dick before."

"Hey, leave me out of this!" Grady was heard weakly protesting.

"Okay everyone, so you all heard what Grady just said. We know incest isn't legal anyway, so since Grady can't legally suck me off, we'll go the next best route; meaning of course, self-service."

And then, while Tommy Burke goggled in disbelief, his 'daughter' bent herself over almost double on the hood of the blue car, took the head of her penis into her mouth and began loudly fellating herself.

"Ugh, sis, that's just gross," Grady protested onscreen. "How can you do that?"

Tommy meanwhile, just looked away, all thoughts of mob money and monstrous mystic manuscripts suddenly very far from his mind.

Tommy didn't consider it safe to look at his laptop again until the scandalous self-sucking sounds stopped.

"Yes, self-service feels fantastic," Kayla was saying, now lying back on the hood and windscreen, and with her spit-wet penis sticking up proudly. "I assure you all that my cock tastes delicious and sweaty; and I've got sweet vanilla salty balls too. So, now let's all come together," she instructed her viewers and then resuming stroking herself. "Oh, my God, guys, see how hard I am now? Oh, wow, I wish you guys were all here so . . ."

For Tommy Burke, watching his daughter first suck on herself and then masturbate also was the absolute limit of things.

Intense rage filled him. Suddenly, the uncharacteristic anger he'd felt on seeing Molly was back again.

The anger felt like someone had opened up his head and poured liquid metal directly into his brain.

Tommy leapt up from his chair. "Okay, that does it," he said aloud. "That sure as hell does it! I'm gonna kill that goddamn whore of a daughter of mine!"

Practically foaming at the mouth now, Tommy lunged towards his office door, with his primary thought being to get to the kitchen, pick up as many knives as he could find, and then hurry upstairs to Kayla's room, knock on her door (she had to still be awake to be posting sleaze at this hour of the night), and then stab her to death with all of those knives as painfully and as messily as he could manage.

But then, just before leaving his office, Tommy managed to calm down and get his wits around him again:

Hey, hey, what's the matter with me? I don't wanna kill Kayla. I LOVE my little girl. Yes, Kayla's a slut, but I've accepted that aspect of her. I dislike her prostituting herself online like that, but . . . hey, what's the matter with me all of a sudden? What the hell has come over me?

Then, with a feeling of horror, Tommy realized what was going on here:

Oh my God! he thought in horror. *It's the book that's making me think these terrible things! It's that book. Just like this morning—the book made me assault Molly and say all that nasty crap to her. And now it's trying to make me kill my own daughter too. Oh my God. Oh my dear God.*

Tommy turned around and stared at his desk.

Just as he'd expected, the book 'How to Succeed in Life' was back in focus on his desk. This time it lay on the wet laptop keyboard, wet from when he'd earlier spilled wine on it.

Tommy could feel the intense rage pouring at him from the horrible little book.

He now understood something else: *The book doesn't want me to murder Kayla for malicious reasons; it wants me to do so to commit me to treading the path of success it's offering within its pages. Kayla's death will merely be a stepping stone to my own greatness.*

And then Grady will be next, of course. To the book's 'mind,' Grady isn't much use to anyone anyway. This way he'll be converted into SUCCESS.

But Tommy wasn't having any of it. He had heard/felt/sensed enough of the book's schemes. With his family being threatened, he was far too angry now to feel fear. He dashed over to his desk, snatched up the book, and then hurried over to the north window of his office and pulled aside the left-hand curtain.

You'll regret this! he thought the book shrilled in his mind as he flung it far out of sight into the night.

He watched as it seemed to soar off like a bird. Then he sagged against the wall, breathing the warm night air in deep, exhaling it long and hard, and then breathing it in deep again, trying to get a hold of himself.

Slowly, he calmed down.

He felt very apprehensive when he looked over at his desk again.

But the book wasn't back again.

However, Tommy Burke wasn't convinced that the evil little skin-bound volume was gone for good.

How right he was.

CHAPTER 28

There, that's done, Kayla though with satisfaction after posting her beach parking lot video. *That'll get me some good likes for sure.*

Indeed, likes and comments were already clicking in from far-off lands where American nighttime was their daylight.

'Wow, honey, you suck your own cock so good! I need to take lessons from you!' fightingsexyboy had just posted from Sweden.

Someone else in Australia had sent her a DM request for a one-on-one webcam session.

Smiling contentedly, Kayla got to her feet. She was thirsty and wanted a glass of water.

Because of the warm night, Kayla had been editing her video in the nude. But now she pulled on her pajamas, in case she ran into her father downstairs.

Pops would freak out for sure. He already keeps going on about how much I look like mom. Seeing me naked at night might be like seeing her ghost.

Kayla was VERY surprised when pulling her pajama pants off of the bed revealed a copy of 'How to Succeed in Life' lying there beneath them.

Hey, I thought Grady took this to the beach with him. Then she frowned. *Hey, hey, hey, what's going on here? Did he sneak back into the house and leave it here again. But no, he couldn't have done. I haven't seen Grady since we got back home. I came in here and have been working ever since. I've not left this room in three hours, so Grady couldn't have brought the book in here.*

They'd gotten back from the beach at 10 p.m., mainly because they'd detoured north to Duxbury to enjoy a seafront dinner.

Once they'd arrived back home, Grady, who'd had one too many drinks and had been wobbling on his feet, had gone straight off to bed.

And he had this book in his hand then. I'm certain of it.

After finding the book in her room during her sex session with Mr. and Mrs. Stainless Strange, Kayla had more or less forgotten about it. Not seeing the book afterwards, she'd assumed her younger brother had simply come back to retrieve it.

But now, here it was again. And by Kayla's simple process of elimination, Grady could not have brought it in here.

Kayla sat down on the bed and picked up the book. Once again, she was struck by how lifelike its texture was.

It's creepy, like holding onto a corpse's hand.

Despite which, she found it difficult to let go of the book. When Grady had suggested that the book might be following him around, she'd laughed it off as a good joke.

But now, Kayla wasn't so sure.

What if this little book does have some powers? I mean, one constantly hears of inexplicable paranormal National-Enquirer type of stuff happening to people.

And then, another thought struck Kayla:

What if there's actually more than one copy of this book?

Kayla flipped through the book's pages, her eyes roving across its lines of indecipherable script, and considered that possibility some more.

Yeah, that'll explain a lot.

The more Kayla thought on it, the more it made sense to her that her brother had found not one, but *two* copies of 'How to Succeed in Life.'

Then her brow creased up again:

But even if there is more than one copy of this, how did this one get in here? No, that's an easy question to answer: Grady somehow forgot one of them here in my room.

Kayla lifted the book up and turned it from side to side to confirm her theory. She opened it up and flipped through its interior.

She decided she was right.

It's like having two small pamphlets, one of which is tucked away inside the other. This book is slim enough for one to make that sort of mistake. I'm, of course, assuming that Grady himself is unaware that there were actually two copies of this book to begin with. But if that's the case, why didn't pops or I notice this when . .
.

From gazing intently at the book's pages but with her mind elsewhere, Kayla Burke suddenly discovered that she understood what she was staring at.

Okay, so I get that part of it . . . Geez, that's bloody. Alright, so . . .

Without being at all aware of her actions, Kayla flipped the book's pale leathery pages back to the beginning and began reading 'How to Succeed in Life' from the top.

CHAPTER 29

Unable to sleep because of persecuting thoughts, Tommy Burke went back to sit at his laptop again.

Thankfully, the laptop no longer showed Kayla masturbating. It was still on her webpage though, prompting him to watch her next video announcing Kayla's upcoming '4 Trans & 2 Man Butthole Bash Orgy' with inset scrolling images of the orgy's participants.

Tommy grimaced at images of three gimpy individuals, and quickly closed Kayla's OnlyFans webpage.

Doing so got his fingers wet and thus reminded him that he'd earlier spilled wine on his laptop keyboard.

Damn!

He got up and looked around his office for something to wipe the keyboard with. Coming back with a batch of paper towels, he quickly cleaned off the laptop and then sat down again. The wine bottle still held a few swallows of alcohol and Tommy filled his glass with this, but didn't immediately drink it.

He felt very disoriented now, and didn't understand why this was.

The book's gone, thank heavens! And I don't have to watch Kayla anymore. Why the hell I clicked on that email notification of hers, I'll never understand.

Tommy put his laptop to sleep.

Alright, this is more than enough for tonight. I've finished Marko's transfers and . . .

Tommy Burke was so enfolded in thought while his laptop powered down that he didn't notice three things: first, that the book 'How to Succeed in Life' was back in his office again; second, that he'd just unwittingly set down his wineglass on it; and third, that while his attention was on other things, a black goo was seeping out of the book.

The emerging black goo swirled itself around the stem of the wineglass and rose quickly upward, until it finally seeped through the bottom of the glass itself and into Tommy's wine.

Once all inside the wine, the black substance twisted and expanded like it was alive for a few seconds, and then it completely dissolved.

"Time for bed," Tommy told himself aloud, reaching for his glass of wine. "Hopefully I've seen the last of that damn—"

As his fingers circled the wineglass, he noticed what the glass stood on.

Holy crap, it's back!

This time Tommy managed not to spill his drink. Still, feeling horrified, he staggered back across the room, until his back hit the far wall.

There, with eyes goggling like mad, and his heart pounding fit to burst, he raised the glass to his lips and drained it in one long gulp.

Only after drinking it all down did Tommy notice the weird aftertaste it left in his mouth. But he didn't pay much attention to this. He was too frightened by the book on the table.

Then slowly, recalling how the book had tried to get him to murder his children, his fright condensed into anger and he scowled at the skin-wrapped little volume.

"Oh, so you don't wanna go, huh?" he told the book, now walking toward it menacingly, like it was a boxing or MMA opponent. "We'll see about that. We'll see how resilient you are when I throw you in the oven and turn on the hea—"

And that was as far as Tommy Burke got before the pain hit him.

The pain exploded inside his belly as if he'd somehow swallowed a grenade with the firing pin removed. It was that intense.

The initial agony was such that Tommy couldn't even cry out. He grabbed his belly with both hands and tried to scream, but the pain rushed up his throat instead. Meanwhile, he could feel his insides twisting as if his guts had suddenly come alive.

It feels like there's a nest of snakes inside me, he thought as now he went down to his knees on the rug.

A further wrench of pain twisted his body around and then dropped him fully to the floor, leaving him sitting with his back to the wall, with his eyes bugging out and the skin on his belly splitting open.

Unable to comprehend what was going on, Tommy pulled up his tee shirt to view his abdomen. In more than one place, its skin was separating as if someone was slicing it open with a knife. And underneath this opening up, the muscles rolled like ocean waves in a thunderstorm.

Crazily though, there was hardly any blood in evidence. His torso seemed to be metamorphosing, not deconstructing.

Tommy more-or-less fainted when his belly finally opened up like a flower.

When he roused, he at first thought he was hallucinating.

Snakes, no no snakes—these are leeches! Tommy thought in a state of delirium. *But no, leeches don't have teeth like this! Oh, my dear God, what the hell is happening to me?*

Tommy had awoken to find himself surrounded by seemingly a forest of two-foot-high snakes.

No, they're worms, he finally decided, considering the fact that their bodies were quite segmented.

He could no longer think clearly. The pain had become his personal universe. It radiated in waves from the center of his body, and became . . . seemingly the pain became the worms.

This of course, was impossible and Tommy rejected the suggestion.

The 'worms' wavered around Tommy, swaying in close to him and then swaying out again. They were eyeless but as Tommy had quickly noticed, their mouths were filled with teeth. They acted like they were hungry; the way they kept moving towards him and snapping their teeth at him, though not attacking him yet.

A quick count revealed there were fifteen or sixteen of them.

Tommy Burke now made the craziest discovery of all:

The worms—Oh God, no—they're not really worms at all, they're my intestines!

And indeed, this was correct. Tommy's intestines really had become the worms. His guts had all uncoiled out of his belly, split into shorter lengths, and been transformed into the horrible creatures that now swayed hungrily around him.

On understanding this ultimate horror, Tommy looked over at the book on his work desk.

The book did this, it fucked up my body like this because I refused to do what it wanted!

But there was much greater horror to come for Tommy Burke.

All of a sudden, one of the longest and thickest intestine-worms struck like a snake at Tommy's face.

Tommy felt a blinding pain in his left eye along with an instant corresponding loss of vision as the worm's mouth completely covered the eye socket. He immediately grabbed at the worm to pull it off of his head. But the thing was both too slimy to get a good grip on and too deeply anchored into his face. And in addition, tugging on it served him up a fresh burst of agony from his torso, which served to remind Tommy that the thing attacking him was after all himself.

The pain in his eye persisted and then his left eye felt like it was exploding.

Tommy discovered he was now completely blind in that eye, and a few seconds later he understood why this was. The intestine-worm that had attacked him now had his left eye in its mouth and was chewing the eye to shreds with its teeth. The intestine-worm dripped with blood and eye jelly.

This can't be happening to me! I'm having the world's most effed-up nightmare.

And his nightmare was already getting much worse. As if spurred on by the 'success' of their large peer, all of the other worms that had metamorphosed from Tommy's intestines now attacked him at once. He felt a cascade of thudding shocks as they all struck him and dug their razorlike teeth into his flesh with fast corkscrewing motions.

One intestine-worm was tunneling into his chest, several were stripping the flesh from his thighs.

One worm was pulling his right ear off of his head. In bright gushes of blood, half of the ear come free. The worm gulped this down and instantly struck again for the other half.

Immediately the worms attacked him en-masse, Tommy had instinctively flung up his right hand to prevent the loss of his right eye also. This defensive move had effectively made him blind, but not for very long. Two worms attached themselves to his covering hand and rapidly stripped the flesh off of the back of it, so that in mere seconds, Tommy was staring through the bones of his hand at the incredible personal monsters that were eating him.

He was floating in a place beyond pain. He had no words—no, no thoughts even—to describe what was happening to him.

How could anyone mentally comprehend that his own body was eating him up and yet remain sane?

However, Tommy remained very aware that this was all the book's doing. Tommy knew that the book 'How to Succeed in Life' was punishing him, that it was showing him that there were worse things than failure to be feared.

Horror of horrors, two of Tommy's worms tore their way through his shorts and began eating up his penis and scrotum.

Unable to scream, Tommy had at least so far managed to keep his mouth shut. But even this didn't last long.

For a while, several worms had been eating away at his face, wolfing down the skin and flesh of his jaws. Suddenly, the muscles that worked his lower jaw were all gone and his mouth fell open of its own accord.

Now, Tommy wished he could scream, because the moment his mouth opened up like this, a long and fat intestine-worm streaked into it and latched itself firmly on his tongue.

Tommy felt crazed. The worm was inside his mouth and his tongue was inside the worm's mouth. And the worm was grinding his tongue down to paste and blood was flooding out of Tommy's face, which was mostly holes now anyway.

It was at this point that Tommy Burke began thinking that, considering what was happening to him, he'd already been alive for way too long.

Fortunately for him, Death apparently agreed. Tommy died seconds after this morbid thought occurred to him.

But even though they were still connected to Tommy's body and were thus a part of him and should have died when he did, the worms that Tommy Burke's intestines had become didn't stop eating him until they were each stuffed full of him and had no more space inside themselves to feed more of him to.

Only then did they all drop to the floor, in the process becoming ordinary lengths of gut again, though still writhing with pleasure from being packed full of bits of Tommy's body.

And then, its evil work done, the book on Tommy's desk vanished for good.

CHAPTER 30

The more Kayla read into 'How to Succeed in Life,' the more horrified she became, the more frightened and revolted, and the more terrified.

She felt like she was stuck in a trance, but at the same time was aware of being thus held captive.

She read on and on and on, unable to stop herself from perusing what seemed to be a lengthy and possibly endless catalogue of atrocious actions. Thoughts and images flowed in sequences through her mind, sometimes linearly, sometimes parallel to each another, sometimes compressed, and at times jumbled up into sensible nonsense.

Kayla read and trembled and almost shat herself from fear.

And then suddenly it was over. The trance broke as abruptly as if someone had shoved a jar of smelling salts under her nose.

What the . . . ?

Kayla stared down at the book in terror.

I don't believe . . . I don't be—

The most scary thing of all, was that she couldn't remember a thing of what she'd just read.

Now very frightened, Kayla dropped the book on her bed again. Then she leapt to her feet and hurried downstairs to get herself a glass of water.

CHAPTER 31

After she'd drank some water, Kayla walked out of the kitchen and stood in the downstairs hallway.

She was indecisive. The unremembered horrors of the book haunted her and made her scared of going back to her bedroom.

Aw c'mon, girl, it's just creepy horror fiction. You're hallucinating. You most likely made all of that evil stuff up yourself.

But Kayla didn't believe her own excuse, and for the simple reason that at no time in her life had she ever had such disgusting thoughts before. Not ever.

And I can't even remember what disgusted me so much!

So, she stood there, trying to get some courage together so she could return to her room, and then throw her copy of 'How to Succeed in Life' into the trash. (She was now convinced that Grady had found more than one copy of the book.)

I don't want that nasty thing anywhere near me. I'm taking it down to the street corner and throwing it into Mike and Tammy's dumpster. I don't care that it's past midnight now.

However, before Kayla Burke could get her courage up enough to carry out what she had in mind, she began hearing noises coming from her father's office.

Then, as she paid close attention to the sounds that she was hearing, she realized that she'd been hearing those same sounds since she came out of the kitchen; possibly even since she'd fled her bedroom. She'd simply been too wrapped up in her fears to pay proper attention to them.

It wasn't unusual for Kayla's father to work this late, and there had been countless times in the past when she'd heard him up at this hour—it was almost 1 a.m. now.

But those sounds are odd, she considered in bemusement. *They're not his classical rock music, or those beepy computer noises because he blew out the left speaker of his laptop and refuses to take it in for repairs or replacement. These sounds are slurpy, like ten or twenty people are eating ice cream in there at once.*

Odd as the weird noises were and creepy as they were too (considering the time of night and the fact that she was standing in an unlight passageway), Kayla nonetheless welcomed the distraction the unfamiliar sounds presented her with. Anything that delayed her return to her bedroom and the evil book was welcome.

So, unaware that what awaited her at the end of her short walk was much worse than what she was avoiding, Kayla Burke headed boldly for her father's office and knocked on his office door.

"Pops? Pops? What's that odd noise? What are you doing in there?"

When her repeated knocks and inquiries brought no response, Kayla calmly opened the door to her father's office.

Then, standing there in the office doorway, and feeling faint as blood drained from her face and disbelief filled her mind, Kayla Burke tried to reconcile the savaged messy corpse on the floor of her father's office with the Tommy Burke that she knew and loved.

Oh, no! That can't be pops! THAT CAN'T BE!

Already on edge because of the evil book she had upstairs in her bedroom, Kayla looked around the office as if this was all just a Halloween-style prank and her father was hiding somewhere nearby and would jump out all of a sudden to scare her.

But finally she was forced to return her gaze to the terrible thing on the floor; the bloody flesh-stripped thing that was clearly the remains of her beloved father; the bloody thing with the exploded belly, outside of which hideously swollen intestines squirmed like they were alive; the thing that had more than half of its flesh missing and from which blood extended in all directions like the tentacles of a liquid red octopus; the thing that had no face and hardly any flesh left on its head except for its surviving right eye, the eye that gaped between the skeleton fingers of the hand that had protected it.

Since stepping inside of her father's office, a scream had been welling up inside of Kayla, a scream that had been prevented from expression only because she'd kept noticing additional macabre details in this terrible scene that faced her.

That scream exploded now from Kayla's throat and entire body and rose to an impossibly loud crescendo, one that travelled far across the neighborhood her family lived in.

And then, once she'd given full vent to her horror, Kayla collapsed in a faint in the doorway of her father's office.

She was still unconscious when, summoned by their neighbors, law enforcement arrived and woke Grady up from his drunken slumber.

Far overhead, the dim lightbulb moon shone down on the world.

CHAPTER 32

The next day at Bundy's Pizzas, Gina listened to Grady's phoned-in horror story in shocked silence.

Finally, she whispered, "Sure," into the mouthpiece of the phone, lowered it to the cradle, and turned to stare at her two bosses, who were again taking inventory at the front counter before the pizza shop opened for the day's business.

"Grady just said to tell you that he won't be in to work today because something killed his father last night and his house is swarming with cops," she told her employers in a quavering voice.

Joe and Susan Bundy gave her equally shocked stares.

"Wha-what d-d-do you mean—*something?*" Susan finally asked, with her brother nodding his agreement with her question. "Like he had an accident at home or something like that?"

Gina shook her head. "No, it wasn't an accident. According to Grady, maybe a bear got into their home."

"Nah, that's absurd," Joe instantly retorted. "Rayham's too far east for that. Never seen a bear over here in my life."

"So . . . go on, go on," Susan prompted. "What else did Grady say?"

Gina nodded nervously and continued: "He said he heard loud banging on the front door of his house at about 1:30 a.m. which woke him up. Apparently, he'd been out drinking with friends and had slept off once he got back home. The noise at the front door turned out to be the cops, who were investigating a loud scream from Grady's house that their next-door neighbor had called in, which turned out to be his sister Kayla, who was found unconscious in the doorway of his dad's office."

Gina swallowed uneasily and looked sick, and then she added: "From what Grady said, something had *eaten* his dad Tommy."

"Eaten?" Susan asked while Joe pulled out a damp handkerchief from his pocket and began dabbing sweat from his round face.

Gina nodded. "Yeah, *eaten*. He was *eaten*, boss. Most of his skin and flesh had been stripped off of his bones to the point where a large amount of him was just skeleton."

"Oh God, no!" Susan exclaimed.

Gina nodded. "Yes, that's what Grady said. He said the police are still trying to figure out how the animal that killed Tommy—which they still think was a bear—got into the house, cuz all the doors were confirmed to have been locked from the inside."

"That sounds crazy," Joe Bundy said, while still mopping up sweat from his brow. "What the hell is the world coming to?"

Susan nodded at her brother. "Yeah, right?" Then she turned back to Gina. "I'm with Joe here; it couldn't have been a bear that did that to Tommy Burke."

"Grady doesn't think so either," Gina agreed. "There's one more detail that he told me."

"What!?" both of her overweight employers enquired at once.

Gina frowned now. "Well, according to him, although his dad's body was totally torn up and there was blood everywhere around him, there were no bloody footprints or handprints of any kind in his dad's office. Not on the walls, or floors, or windows. Nothing of the sort."

"Nah, c'mon, that's impossible," Joe said, finally putting his handkerchief back into his pocket. "What're they trying to imply— that Tommy Burke was killed by a ghost?"

Gina shrugged. "Boss, I dunno, I'm just reporting what was told to me. Grady says that whatever creature killed his dad, arrived in their home, ate him, and left without leaving any traces of its coming or going. Right now as we speak, forensics are going over their place with toothcombs, searching for clues."

CHAPTER 33

Grady's creepy phone call had cast a somber shadow over Gina.

However, once the pizza shop opened for that Sunday's business, with the warm smells coming from the kitchen in back and the occasional customers coming in the front door, Gina was able to forget why Grady wasn't coming in to work today.

When she did think about Grady, she thought of how horrible it must be to lose both of one's parents.

Damn, his mother died of cancer a few years ago and now this?

Both of Gina's own parents were still alive and Gina resolved to call them once she finished work for the day.

Her thoughts then returned to Grady Burke:

Grady is certain to be feeling lonely now. Oh, I just wish I could comfort him. A dreamy smile lit up her face. *Cuz I know he's totally into me, but he's just not go-getter enough. Joe Bundy is more my style of man. Yeah, yeah, he's FAT as a hog, but he's got drive—which handsome Grady lacks in spades. Alright, so I'm currently entangled with Joe's sister, but for a while now Joe's been subtly letting me know that he's available once my romantic lease with Susan has run out, cuz he don't want to hurt her. But still, I may have to start comforting Grady on the side, just to ensure he doesn't commit suicide from depression . . . Even on a good day, Grady looks like he needs comforting—like he jerks off a lot and needs a loving female shoulder to cry on . . .*

It was now that Gina became aware of the man standing beside the counter. Noticing him felt like she was emerging from a trance.

Because he's standing directly opposite me and I didn't even realize he'd come into the shop. Geez, Gina, hold it together. You can't get wrapped up in thoughts like this.

The man was standing patiently there. He had a strange face, like all the strange faces that Gina had ever seen rolled into one. Staring at him made her feel weird.

"Would like to order a pizza?" she asked while feeling like spiders were walking down her back and up her thighs.

The strange man with the strange face smiled a strange smile. "No, thank you. I've a delivery for a Ms. Gina Luz."

"Oh, that's me," Gina said in surprise. "What did you bring me?"

Then she saw that he was holding out a package to her.

Now, she wasn't sure how long he'd had the package in his hand. Had he been holding onto it all along? Or did it just appear when she confirmed her identity to him? The latter alternative seemed the actuality of things, but sanity and logic dictated that the former was what must have occurred.

"Well, here you are, miss," the man said.

Her fingers trembling, Gina accepted the package from the smiling man and examined it. Wrapped in regular brown paper, the package was small and flexible.

Oh, it's a book of some kind, she thought.

She looked up again and asked: "Okay, where do I sign for it?"

But now Gina saw that she was all alone in the pizza shop. She could hear activity in the back, and smell food cooking, but out here in front? She was the only one here, except if one counted the two teenagers who were walking past the deli on the opposite side of the highway.

Gina did a double-take and then hurried out from behind the service counter to check that the courier man wasn't crouching down in front of it.

But there was no one there. Gina was all alone here in the front room of the pizza shop.

She felt scared and covered in gooseflesh. She tried to figure out how the man could have left the shop without her noticing him . . . because . . . she had a clear view left and right all the way out to the highway, and the pizza shop parking lot was empty too.

Huh? Did I just hallucinate? Did I just imagine all of that?

But, looking down again, Gina confirmed that she couldn't have imagined the man being in here with her.

She still had the package he'd brought her.

She began unwrapping it. She now realized for the first time that the little package simply had 'GINA'S COPY' handwritten on it; no address or anything else.

Once she'd slipped the content from the package, Gina was confused again:

Huh? It's another copy of 'How to Succeed in Life.' The same book that Susan has, which Katie said a customer forgot in here. Yes, it's exactly the same one: same freakish leather like human skin, same nonsensical writing outside and in.

But Gina's confusion didn't extend to the reason *why* she was receiving a copy of the book:

It's cuz I was thinking of Grady Burke just now. Yeah, I'm getting this book because I was thinking of comforting Grady Burke!

And on that realization, almost as if someone had flicked a switch somewhere to freeze time while the vanished man made his arcane delivery to Gina Luz and then his subsequent getaway, the pizza shop phone began ringing, Joe Bundy emerged from the rear with a stack of hot pizzas, Jimmy Hutch and Megan Brooks both drove their cars into the parking lot, and Gina was once more occupied with work.

CHAPTER 34

Tommy Burke's funeral took place the next Friday, a cold and miserable day like the sun was striking for higher pay and had put summer on hold until its work demands were met.

Considering the state of Tommy's body, no one had objected to his being cremated.

In the meantime, the coroner's office had ruled the cause of Tommy Burke's death as 'Inexplicable Spontaneous Auto-Consumption,' a variation of the terms used for folks who, without being set on fire, burst into flames on their own and burnt to death.

In their case the term used was 'Spontaneous Auto-Combustion.'

It had been firmly established by forensics that Tommy Burke had not been killed by a bear or any other animal known to man, or by a man or woman for that matter.

And the coroners still couldn't explain how all the flesh that had been stripped from Tommy's face and body—every single chunk of it—was packed inside of his own intestines.

"It's as crazy as if his own intestines ate him up," one coroner guy told another.

So 'Spontaneous Auto-Consumption,' was the verdict.

Anyway, that overcast Friday morning, Tommy Burke's funeral service was held at the Sowiecki Funeral Home in the abutting town of Taunton.

CHAPTER 35

After the funeral service, Grady stood with Ricky out in the parking lot of the Sowiecki Funeral Home, greeting and thanking the attendees.

"Pop's funeral was well attended," Grady observed during one interlude between greetings. "He sure had lots of friends."

"Yeah," Ricky agreed. "But some of 'em look real shady."

Grady nodded. "If you mean that group Kayla's with at the moment, you're right."

In her black mourning outfit, today Kayla looked beautiful and serene and yet supremely miserable. She was over on the opposite side of the parking lot, talking to a small group of men and women.

"That's Marko Velli and the Boston mob," Grady further explained.

Grady caught sight of Kayla waving to them and nudged Ricky with his elbow. "C'mon, let's go join the mob."

As they walked, Grady pulled out the vape pen he'd now permanently borrowed from Kayla and took a quick puff of THC.

"Hey, you'd better be careful with that stuff," Ricky warned as Grady put the vape pen away in his suit jacket again. "You're turning into a pothead on us all."

Grady gave Ricky a mellow smile. "Dude, it's the only way I've been able to cope with things this week. Cuz half the time I'm unsure what I'm seeing around our house, you know?"

Grady had been stoned for the past five days. Not stoned 24/7, but he'd been on Planet Reggae for half of that time. The only times Grady hadn't been high this week was when he was driving around delivering pizzas and when he was asleep.

Grady missed Tommy badly. His father's death had hit him much worse than losing his mother had.

There were two reasons for this: Firstly, because Helen Burke had had cancer for almost a year before dying, and so her family had gotten used to the fact of her exit from this life before she quit it. Secondly, Tommy had still been around after Helen's passing; Grady and Kayla had still had one parent to sooth their sorrows over the exit of the other.

But now, both siblings were all alone.

First mom was gone and now pops is gone too and it's just us both left.

CHAPTER 36

Marko Velli was a stocky middle-aged man with a smile that never really reached his eyes. Grady knew the man was a mobster because Kayla was good friends with Danny Foster, who was the boyfriend of Sluggo Lakes, one of the kingpin's right-hand men. Sluggo and Danny had been at the funeral service, but were absent from the group now.

"I'm so, so sorry this had to happen to you kids," Marko told Grady after shaking hands with him and Ricky. "Your father was a very close business associate of mine."

"Thank you for coming today, sir," Grady replied sincerely. He was still surprised that the Boston crime kingpin was here for his dad's funeral.

Marko smiled paternally at Grady and Kayla. "Now, you kids may not know this, but your dad had some investments." Marko stopped talking and snapped his fingers at a skeletally thin man whose eyes were hidden behind black glasses. "Hey, Horowitz, did ya bring the papers with you?"

"Yeah, got 'em in the car, boss."

Satisfied by the man's reply, Marko returned his attention to the two bereaved siblings. "I understand you'll be having a short reception at your house now. You're gonna have to excuse me from that, cuz I've an appointment back in Boston in forty-five minutes, but Horowitz here will explain to you what sort of financial legacy your pop left to you two." Marko smiled his smile that didn't reach his eyes again. "Lemme put it this way—neither of you really need to work for a living again."

Grady and Kayla both stared at each other and then at Marko Velli.

"Really?" Kayla finally asked.

Marko nodded. "Yeah. Your dad was a stand-up guy. He made arrangements to have you both well-catered for if anything happened to him." Then after a glance at his wristwatch, Marko Velli laid a hand on each of their shoulders. "Listen, kids, I really gotta go. Look me up whenever you're in Boston." Then he smiled at Grady. "Son, you know anything about bitcoins and crypto dealing?"

Grady shook his head. "No, sir. Nothing at all."

Marko nodded. "Well, look it up, okay? You never know when the knowledge will come in handy."

And then Marko shook hands with everyone and departed with his entourage.

Grady stared after the departing mobster, and then looked at his sister.

"Did you hear what he said?"

Kayla smiled thinly. "I sure did. I don't believe we won't need to work again, but it's sweet of Mr. Velli to tell us that." Then she frowned at Grady. "Listen, little brother, stop vaping at our daddy's funeral. There's no bogeymen here that are gonna get ya. They're all hiding in the closet back at home."

While Grady sought a suitable reply to this, Kayla turned on Ricky also: "And, you, where's that little witch of yours? Huh, where is Molly? Where is she?"

Ricky cringed. "Molly couldn't make it here. She's working today."

Kayla leaned close enough to Ricky that she could have licked his face, and whispered: "Yes, that's right, she's working. Your little witch is probably sucking someone else's dick and then she'll steal their wallet and ID too. But listen, I know she's the one who killed my daddy."

"Hey, Kayla, c'mon—" Ricky began protesting, but Kayla silenced him with a finger pressed firmly against his lips.

"Molly said she'd tell her aunt to hex pops and that he'd die a miserable and a painful death, didn't she?" Kayla asked, still in that horrible whisper like a dying crone's rasping voice. "And that same fucking night it happened, didn't it? I swear, once I get my hands on her, that beating pops gave her will be nothing compared to what I'll—"

Grady chose that moment to flee. Kayla was still whispering at Ricky, but Grady didn't want to be around her if she upgraded her expression of her anger to a shouting match.

Thankfully, he'd just seen Susan Bundy and Gina emerge from a group of people, and hurried over there to talk to them.

"I'm really sorry for your loss," Susan told Grady. "I can't come to the house for the reception—gotta head back to the pizza shop. Joe sends his condolences too."

Grady nodded. "Thanks to you both. I dunno how I'd have survived this week without the support of all of you."

Gina leaned forward and kissed him on the cheek. "I'm sorry too, man. It was really horrible what happened to your dad."

Grady nodded. "Yeah, it was. Thanks for coming, both of you."

"Gimme a call if you need to discuss anything," Gina said, afterwards kissing his cheek again.

Grady felt warmed that she was so concerned about him. He was about replying that he would call her, then he saw the possessive look on Susan's face and decided against it.

Best to let scissoring pussies lie.

As the two women walked off, Grady looked around the parking lot of the funeral home. The crowd was thinning out, with some people driving back to work, and others driving over to Kayla and Grady's house for the funeral reception, which was being hosted by Danny Foster.

Grady glanced back over at Kayla. She'd now left Ricky alone, because they'd been joined by a group of her friends.

Grady recognized some of her friends. Danny Foster and his boyfriend Sluggo Lakes were there amongst them, along with a good number of Kayla's porno friends.

He heard Danny and Sluggo telling the others that they were leaving for the house to take care of the guests.

Seeing as his sister wasn't looking his way at the moment, Grady took a quick hit of THC.

Grady wondered which two of Kayla's friends that he didn't recognize were the normally latex-covered Mr. and Mrs. Stainless Strange.

Then Ricky escaped from Kayla's porno group and hurried over to Grady's side.

"Thanks for ditching me back there, dude," Ricky told Grady. "You're a friend in need indeed."

Grady smiled, feeling mellow from the vape smoke. "Dude, what can I say? Sis has held Molly responsible for pops' death since day one. I'm just relieved she didn't tell that to the cops."

"I'm glad I didn't bring Molly to the funeral."

Grady nodded back at him. "Glad? Dude, I'm positively delighted you left Molly at home. Cuz, the way Kayla's been going on about her for the past week, she'd have ripped your sweetheart to pieces in front of everyone if Molly had been attendance here."

"I know your sister's given to theatrics, but that'd be overkill even for her."

Grady frowned at Ricky. "C'mon, bro, what do you expect Kayla to think? We all heard Molly say she'd call up her aunt to curse pops. And . . . and you yourself saw pops' body in the morgue—Dude, what the hell could've done that to him? Put his own flesh in his own guts like that, except some magic spell?"

Ricky looked confused. "Yeah, yeah, I'm not disputing that there's something paranormal about this, but here's the thing: Molly swears she had nothing to do with it. I already told you this, didn't I? Molly swears she didn't curse your dad or ask her psychic aunt to do it."

Grady looked confused. "Well, I'm not saying I believe she did curse pops, but . . ."

Ricky quickly went on: "Listen, dude, why would Molly go to all that trouble just to get even with your pop? We all went to the beach together, didn't we? And you, Kayla, and I all saw that Molly was *happy*, blissfully happy when we were driving home."

Grady thought on that for a moment. "Okay, okay. But were you together all through that night?"

Ricky shook his head. "No, I dropped her off at her sister's place." He frowned. "Okay, I see what you're getting at. Conceivably, Molly could've had a change of heart after I dropped her off, maybe at her sister's urging, cuz, man, Janie *was* mad about the puffy state of Molly's face and . . ." Ricky made a face. "No, no, no—she's nothing like that. Okay, so sometimes Molly lies and maybe she'd steal from you, but she's not malicious like that. Not to the point of committing a supernatural murder. No, no, she's not that kind of girl."

"Don't sweat it, dude, I believe you," Grady told Ricky. Then he nodded over at his sister who was now getting into a car and was waving at them both to hurry over. "We just need to convince *her* of your girl's innocence."

CHAPTER 37

"So, how's it feel to be like, rich?" Kayla asked Grady.

"I dunno, I'm waiting till everything passes the courts and we actually get the money," was his stoned reply.

It was Saturday, the day after Tommy Burke's funeral. Brother and sister were sitting in their living room getting high on some new vape cartridges that Kayla had just bought. The legal papers that Mr. Horowitz had handed them yesterday lay scattered across the coffee table.

"I never even suspected pops had so much money," Kayla said. "One-and-a-half million dollars? I wonder how he earned that much?"

"Who cares, sis?"

"Yeah, bro, who fucking cares?"

Grady took a hit from the vape pen and then passed it across to Kayla.

"So what you gonna do with your half of our windfall?" asked Kayla while exhaling pale smoke from her nostrils.

"I'm figuring I'd like to go back to university for a master's degree . . . in whatever."

"Yeah, 'whatever' sounds like a really good course to study."

"What you gonna do now, sis?"

Kayla grinned broadly. "I dunno yet. Maybe I'll do like you and go back to school. Or maybe I'll set up a business selling personalized sex toys. Actually, I can do both—sell my own line of sex toys while attending university."

"Not a bad idea. But for the moment, I gotta continue working at the pizza place."

"What for?"

Grady smiled. "Well, I think Gina likes me. I may get some sympathy sex out of pops' death."

"Hmmm. Isn't Gina a dyke?"

"Not sure she's sure herself."

"Well, best of fuck with getting in where it's tight and wet."

Then Kayla sighed deeply and looked concerned.

"What's the matter?" Grady asked her.

"I just remembered that tomorrow, Sunday, is the date for my '4 Trans & 2 Man Butthole Bash Orgy.' "

"You still wanna do that?"

Kayla shook her head. "I don't really have a choice. I don't really wanna do a sex show so soon after pops's death, but I've advertised the Butthole Bash Orgy for a full month now, and the interest level is up in the clouds. This show will likely break the sexual internet."

"Okay . . ."

"But this is my *last* fucking show. For real. I don't think I wanna do porn any longer. I'm quitting in honor of pops' memory."

"Pops would've loved that and so I support your resolve and resolution," Grady replied. Then after taking a hit of vape smoke and peering intently at an old portrait of their family that hung on the opposite wall, he smiled at Kayla and added: "It's just like pops used to say: you really do look like mom does in those old wedding photos."

Kayla sighed. "Don't you start. Pops sometimes had me feeling like I committed identity theft by becoming a woman."

"Whatever. He loved you. Pops really loved us both."

"Yeah, whatever. I really loved pops too. May his soul rest in perfect peace."

"Amen to that."

Then Grady frowned. "Sis, did we bring the damn evil book downstairs with the inheritance papers?"

Kayla looked over at the coffee table, saw the book lying on top of the mentioned documents, and frowned. "I didn't. Did you?"

"I don't remember doing so, but I guess I might have." He waved the vape pen at her. This is some bomb-ass canna, so just about everything's possible."

Brother and sister both stared at the little book.

"You know," Grady said after a little while. "Yesterday, Ricky suggested that pops' death might be somehow connected to this book being in our possession."

Kayla snorted smoke like a dragon. "Really? He really said that?"

"Grady nodded. "Yep. At the time we were both drunk, so I laughed it off, but now that I'm stoned I'm starting to think he might have a point."

Kayla began laughing. "You're both dumbasses. How in the hell can this little book have killed our daddy? He didn't even have a copy. Just you and I do."

Grady looked at Kayla. "You've got a copy too?"

She nodded back at him. "Yeah, You brought two home that day, not one."

"I coulda sworn it was just one."

"It wasn't, kiddo. Two for sure."

"Oh, whatever."

"Yeah, whatever. Far as I'm concerned, daddy's death was all Molly's work. The witch put a hex on pops and that's what killed him. Don't it strike you as fishy that he died exactly how she predicted he would? With his belly exploding and all of that?"

Grady nodded. "I guess." Then he frowned at his sister. "Let's not argue about it. Pass the vaper."

Kayla handed it over. "It sure is great being rich though."

Grady frowned. "Ask me 'bout it after I get the money."

CHAPTER 38

While driving to work on Sunday afternoon, Grady found himself looking forward to seeing Gina Luz.

What the hell do I wanna see her for anyway? Grady asked himself. *Am I seriously gonna try for those sympathy fucks like I told Kayla?*

Grady laughed and turned his black Toyota Camry off the highway and into the Bundy's Pizzas parking lot. No, he wasn't about attempting to seduce Gina.

I wouldn't dare hurt Susan like that.

Nonetheless, the memory of Gina's soft lips pressed against his cheek when she'd kissed him brought a warm smile to his lips.

But . . . she did seem genuinely sympathetic at pops' funeral, like maybe she's someone I can talk to 'bout how I feel now.

Grady parked his car and headed into the shop.

This afternoon, Katie Jensen, a small woman with bright red hair, had the first shift at the shop counter instead of Gina.

"Hi, Katie, what's up?" Grady greeted her.

"Definitely not Bundy's Pizzas, Katie replied pleasantly, then asked: "Your nose notice anything weird in here today?"

Grady sniffed the air for a bit. "Hey, I don't smell any pizzas cooking." This Sunday afternoon those normal delightful odors of baking pastry and cooking fillings were mournfully absent in the front shop/restaurant.

Katie nodded. "Yup, that's it. Something is wrong with the gas feeds to the kitchen, and I think with the electricity too. None of the ovens is working and none the ranges either. Joe called the company that installed them, but their repair team can't make it here till tomorrow, Monday."

"So, we've no deliveries to make?"

Katie shook her head. "None yet anyway. But you can't leave yet. Joe says he's called someone else to come have a look at the gas fault, but even so, it'll take *them* a couple hours to get here. And with no cooking happening for the moment, Susan has since departed for parts unknown."

"Parts unknown?" Grady asked helplessly.

Katie laughed. "Well, she didn't let me know where she was going anyway. But I'm certain Joe knows."

Grady nodded. "No problem. I'll hang around then." Then he asked: "Is Gina here, or did she go out with Susan?"

Katie nodded. "Yeah, Gina's around. We were chatting ten minutes ago, but then the boss called for her."

Grady pondered on this for a few moments. He could either wait out front here for Gina to return, or he could go look for her. The thing was, seeing that, as Susan's lover, Gina practically lived in the rear of the pizza shop, she might go back to Susan's apartment after her meeting with Joe and not come back out front again at all.

And besides . . . I need to take a piss, and the restroom is right next to Joe's office. And this is an opportunity I shouldn't waste. Seeing as there's no work happening at the moment—that gives Gina and I lots of time to chat.

Humming a tune the name of which he didn't remember, Grady made his way back through the building.

After passing the kitchen, which was uncharacteristically silent, Grady backtracked a few paces and peeked inside of it.

The place was empty and quiet. Completely inactive, with just the leftover odors of pizzas already done and delivered present.

Grady opened the kitchen door wide and stared from one gas range to the next, from one end of the immense cooking chamber to the other, at the extensive kitchen islands and the giant gleaming pots and kitchenware and storage vats, and at the huge fridges, shelves, and pallets all stacked up with containers of pizza components and condiments, and at the plastic-protected piles of pizza boxes.

It was strange seeing the place so inactive during the day.

Now it seemed like he was smelling the ghosts of pizzas sold and the ghosts of those pizzas yet to come.

Grady closed the kitchen door, walked a bit further, and then made the left turn that would take him to the staff restroom.

He stepped into the restroom and then heard the door of Joe Bundy's office open up.

Intending to tell Gina to wait up so they could chat, Grady stepped out of the restroom again.

He was surprised to see Gina, who was looking back into Joe's office and as such hadn't yet noticed him, naked from the waist upward. Gina's short hair was quite messed up also. She blew a wet kiss back into the boss's office, and now began pulling her tee shirt down over her head.

"You know, someone might see ya out there," Joe said from inside the office.

Gina shook her hair back into place and finger-combed it. "No one but Katie is around." She laughed. "Baby, that was just so smart of you: disconnecting the gas feeds to the kitchen like that and then telling poor Susan that they're all clogged and that the repair guys can't get here until Monday."

"Susan's happy enough. There's some business she's been wanting to look into anyway, but never had the time cuz she doesn't trust leaving the pizza-making to just me; you know how she's always complaining that I use too much cheese and not enough sausage. Anyway, once I cut the gas supply and diddled with the electric fuses too, she decided that she'd go visit our shop in Fall River to sort out those quality control issues we're having with the cooks there. We've been getting all sorts of complaints from that joint; customers saying the delivery guys or gals ate half their pizzas and the delivery gals and guys claiming the manager is on coke and has been stealing their tips to fund his habit."

Gina laughed. "Susan told me about the cokehead manager. She asked me to come along south to Fall River with her, but I pleaded that I had a headache and couldn't go."

"If Susan ever finds out that I intentionally disconnected the kitchen just so you and I can have some alone time today . . ."

"Man, she won't find out. Who's gonna tell her?"

"Okay," Joe said. Now git, before she either forgets something and comes back looking for it or someone walks into the corridor to take a shit and sees you standing there looking all sexily disheveled like that."

"And *you?*"

"Honey, that was quite the workout you just gave me. I'll get dressed and be outside once I get my breath back. Now shut my office door. I don't want someone walking past and mistaking me for a lump of unkneaded dough."

Gina blew him another kiss and shut the office door.

Then, pulling her cellphone from a pocket of her denim skirt, she began walking towards the rear of the building where the apartments were situated.

"Hey there," Grady told her, seeing that she was already so much into her phone that she'd have walked right past him without noticing he was there.

Gina looked up and saw him standing in the restroom doorway. Her surprise and alarm were immediately both obvious.

"How long have you been standing here?" she asked him. She spoke in a whisper, however, as if suddenly she was afraid of detection.

"Long enough," Grady replied. "Long enough to see more of you than I needed to and to learn more about you than I wanted to."

He watched Gina think on what he'd said for a few seconds, as if trying to make up her mind whether she liked what he meant or not.

Finally, however, she realized she didn't. Her face set in a scowl and her eyes blazed fiercely.

"Well, I sure hope you got yourself a good look at my tits, loser," she spat angrily at him. "Cuz that's the first and last glimpse of them you're ever gonna get."

"Yeah, yeah, that's fine," Grady replied disinterestedly. "I fully understand that love don't pay no bills. But riddle me one answer: what's gonna happen between Joe, Sue, and you when Susan finds out?"

Gina smirked nastily at Grady. "Tell the fat bitch and lose your job."

With that warning or threat hanging in the air, Gina walked off, instantly dipping her gaze back down to study her cellphone, like she'd already forgotten all about Grady.

Grady watched her go. "I guess the pretty lady don't feel like comforting me today," he told himself. And then his own gaze locked onto something shocking.

What's that in the pocket of her skirt? A copy of 'How to Succeed in Life?'

Grady stared hard at the pinkish-brown object sticking out of the left side pocket of Gina's denim skirt. She was just about to exit the hallway, and as such was too far-off for him to be sure that it wasn't actually an envelope or a purse that he could see in her pocket.

However, something about the way the object looked assured him that it was a copy of 'How to Succeed in Life' that Gina had with her.

But then, he shrugged.

It's not worth worrying about, he told himself. *Even if Gina does somehow have a copy of the evil book also, she's too much of an airhead to understand what it's about anyway.*

Suddenly Grady felt very tired of people. As he finally shut himself into the restroom, a worrying thought flashed through his mind:

How many copies of that book are there anyway? And how is it that it's turning up with people close to me?

Then he relaxed a bit. "No, not everyone," he told his reflection in the restroom mirror. "Ricky's my best friend, and *he* hasn't gotten a copy of it yet."

Well, Grady was right about this, but he had no idea of just how dramatically that fact was about to change.

CHAPTER 39

"Okay, baby, so what is it you wanted to talk to me about?" Ricky asked Molly early that same Sunday afternoon.

He and Molly were watching TV in his living room.

Ricky was feeling worried. This was because Molly had been looking worried for about an hour now.

Ricky needed to be at work at the Cashstretch supermarket in two hours, but he knew that he wouldn't concentrate much on work unless he knew exactly what was bothering Molly, who, all of a sudden looked freaked out.

"What on your mind, baby?" Ricky asked her, pulling her in close to him on the couch. "If it's about all that past-life stuff of yours; I already told ya to forget about it. What's past is past."

Molly kissed his cheek. "Well, it is sort of about that."

"Then forget it, like I've already done."

Molly however shook her head. "No, no. It's not the sex thing—there's something else I wanna tell you about."

That surprised Ricky and he pushed her gently away from him and held her at arm's length. "What something else?"

"Okay, it's like this," Molly said. "I already told you I had nothing to do with Grady's dad's death. I didn't ask my aunt to curse her or anything like that."

"Yah, yah, I believe ya," Ricky said. "We've already been over this too."

Molly nodded. "Just listen, baby. What I didn't tell you, is that I couldn't tell my Aunt Melda to hex Mr. Burke even if I wanted to. She died, see?"

Now Ricky frowned. "No, you didn't tell me that. You just said you used to work for her and that she fired you cuz you accused her of being a fake medium."

Molly sighed. "Yeah, that's what I told you. But, baby, I lied."

"Why would you do that?"

"It's because I'm scared to remember what happened to Aunt Melda," Molly said. "See, she didn't die an ordinary sort of death."

She was looking at Ricky with an expectant kind of look.

"Well go on," he prompted her. "Don't kill me with suspense. How *did* your aunt die?"

"She lost her head."

"What?"

Molly nodded. "It's true. The tragedy began when Aunt Melda was invited to perform an exorcism of a house on Carver Street, you know, up in the north part of town.

"Now, first off, I need to stress that Aunt Melda *wasn't* a fraud. She was a genuine medium, and actually did communicate with the other side. I'd been there on more than one occasion when she made contact with spirits—departed human souls, ghosts . . . and whatever.

"Anyhow, in this particular case, I went with Aunt Melda to this supposedly haunted house on Carver Street. The building's 'unseen resident' had been causing the owner of the house no end of misery, so much discomfort in fact that the woman offered Aunt Melda *a lot* of money to cleanse the place for her."

Ricky nodded. "And no one turns down a good payday, right?"

Molly nodded. "You said it, baby. So, we went over there, she and I. It was some old building that the town should've knocked down ages ago. And immediately I set my eyes on it, I recall thinking it was cursed. Once we stepped up on the front porch, Aunt Melda turned to me and told me the house was cursed. I looked at her and said, 'I've a bad feeling 'bout this.' " She told me that she felt the same way."

"You were both certain of that? That that house had a curse, before you'd even performed any rites of exorcism?" Ricky asked.

Molly nodded. "Once you stepped over the front threshold, you could feel it. All of a sudden, the air felt heavier, if that makes any sense to you." Molly wiped her face with the back of her right hand. "I'd almost liken it to visiting a different world, maybe a different planet—you know how gravity is supposed to be different on each planet in the solar system for instance, so that you weigh less on the moon than you do on earth, but you'd weigh more on Mars? Something like that. Anyway, it was freaky; after entering that house, I immediately felt like I'd put on a hundred extra pounds. The atmosphere in the house seemed thicker too. Sure, I could breathe, but I seemed to be breathing in something else in addition to air. And that something, whatever it was, was totally bad.

" 'It's easy to understand why no one wants to live in this place,' Aunt Melda told me. 'I've been here five minutes, haven't seen anything out of the ordinary yet, and I wouldn't live here for half of the oil in Texas.' "

"Go on," Ricky said. "I don't even know what the punchline is and you're already creeping me out."

"Anyway," Molly went on, "the woman who'd hired us was waiting. Her name was Erin De Mornay. So, we went on in with Erin De Mornay, who was attractive in a creepy way. She was either in her late thirties or early middle age. Jet black hair, dark makeup and bright, bright eyes like she was high on darkness or something." Molly shook herself. "But the strange thing about her, was that she didn't strike me as being out of context in that house. On the other hand, I had the feeling that she was personally responsible for making the house into what it was. I mean, seriously. She was dressed in black leather and had on a red tee shirt with a black pentagram drawn on it, along with a goat-head pendant dangling between her breasts on a silver necklace. Her earrings were black upside-down crosses. Fingernails black as coal. As a final eerie detail, in one hand she was holding a creepy book with indecipherable lettering on its cover. In short, Ms. De Mornay looked every inch the modern witch."

"She sounds totally freaky," Ricky said. "Go on."

"So anyway, she led us to the foot of a spiral staircase, pointed up the stairs, and then told us, 'You'll both have to go on alone from here. I'm too scared of the upper floor now to accompany you up there.' Aunt Melda nodded, and I once again had a bad feeling about this, because I could tell she was lying. I knew that Erin De Mornay wasn't scared to go up the stairs; she just didn't want to do so at that particular time. But just like with how I felt our hostess fit in perfectly with her house and all that, I couldn't tell my suspicions to my aunt, because Ms. De Mornay was right there in the room with us." And here Molly smiled sadly, before adding, "I wanted to turn and run away from there. But see, the psychic business hadn't been paying us too well for the past two months, and my rent was overdue."

"So, of course, you went up the stairs," Ricky said.

"Yep, we both climbed that spiral staircase to the upper floor," Molly agreed.

"And what did you find up there?"

Molly shrugged. "Now that the incident is past, I don't really remember everything that was upstairs in that house. However, I do remember this much: Okay, now you remember what I said about Aunt Melda being genuine? So, even before Erin had directed us towards the stairs, she'd been chanting mantras and attempting to get in tune with the house and its spirits. This was another reason why I didn't tell her my suspicions about Erin—I didn't want to ruin her concentration. It was also possibly why Aunt Melda herself didn't suspect that Erin De Mornay was lying to us."

By this point in her narrative, Molly's face had begun reflecting the horror she'd felt back then, and her dread memories were affecting Ricky too.

"So, I remember us reaching the top of the stairs and turning left. Why we went left instead of right, I'm not sure, cuz I don't think Erin directed us either way. Anyway, all of a sudden, we were inside a room. Now I recall another weird detail too: that we didn't seem to walk as much as we needed to, to arrive at the room.

"The room had red walls. Not like red was their original color, but walls that had been painted red afterwards—in strips where the red brush strokes hadn't reached you could still see the original cream paint underneath." Molly wrung her hands together. "Now, I'm not certain if I saw this or not—the police said there was no such thing in the room—but I think there was a dead and rotting baby in the room."

"Shit!" Ricky said.

"The baby hadn't died naturally either," Molly went on. "All of the organs in its torso had been scooped out, its belly had been filled with sand, and a black flower—some kind of tropical flower—had been planted in the sand in its belly."

Ricky's eyes gaped wide. "What the fuck?"

Molly nodded back at him. "Yeah. I really think I saw that, and you can just imagine what the place smelt like with the kid's corpse rotting away in there. But like I said, the cops later told me that the dead and rotting baby wasn't up there, so I may have just hallucinated that part of it." She shivered. "It was that kinda spooky house, the kind that fills one's head with nightmares. The sort of place where you'd wanna hold your Halloween party, expecting the devil to be a guest too."

Ricky nodded. "So . . ."

"So, anyway in the meantime, Aunt Melda is like in a trance. That didn't alarm me, I was used to stuff like that; entering a trance helped her contact her spirit guides. But then, while she's chanting away, I noticed that the wall to her right, near where the baby's corpse was, that area of the wall was bulging outwards and a pair of hands had started poking out of it."

Molly looked at Ricky. Ricky didn't say anything. Molly went on: "Remember that I'm already suspicious of Erin De Mornay, so I'm nervous as a rabbit. So when I see the hands coming out of the wall also grow a pair of arms, I only think the worst. And I now notice that that particular wall of the room doesn't look like a regular wall anymore, its surface has begun throbbing like there are blood vessels beneath it. And worst still, the hands that came out of it weren't regular hands—they're like twice normal human size and end in long black claws. 'Aunt Melda, snap out of it!' I yell at my aunt. But she, of course, doesn't snap out of it at all. She's too deep in her trance, and now only the whites of her eyes are visible in their sockets.

"And meanwhile, the arms extending out of the fleshy wall are revealing that they're connected to a body and the head of that body is coming through too now. The creature emerging from the wall has an animal's head." Lost deep in her recollection, Molly now hugged herself and shivered. "Man, I can't describe what sort of animal head it was—all I saw clearly was that it had horrible long teeth. 'Aunt Melda, snap out of it!' I screamed, certain now that Erin De Mornay hadn't wanted her house cleansed of bad spirits at all, but had simply needed a sacrifice for whatever was coming out of that fleshy wall. And any doubts that I might have had as to that being the case were easily nullified by Erin's own laughter, which I could hear loud and clear now, coming from downstairs." Molly frowned. "Long story short, I tried to force Aunt Melda out of the room, but it felt like she was cemented to the floor.

"The creature was about halfway out of the wall now. In complete horror I watched its left foot break completely free of the flesh-or-skin wall and stamp the floor. That foot had even more claws that its hands did." Molly shuddered. "Now, honey, you need to understand something; this wasn't a slow transition, it was happening really really fast. I did my best to get my aunt out of there—I really really really did. But it was impossible to move her. I was still attempting to get Aunt Melda unstuck and turned around when I heard a loud snapping sound behind me. That was it for me. Without looking back, I realized that the creature—demon, monster, whatever—was now fully in the room with us. At that moment, I let go of Aunt Melda and fled screaming."

Molly was hugging herself hard and shuddering now. "I didn't stop running till I was down at the bottom of the stairs. And down there was Erin De Mornay reading from her creepy book. She was chanting away and laughing.

" 'You set us up,' I immediately accused her.

" 'But you got away,' she replied me with a broad and satisfied smile while I glared at her. 'But that's okay: I didn't really need two sacrifices anyway. Boku Vezek will be satisfied with just your aunt.' And right then, up there on the upper floor I heard my aunt gasp loudly, and then there was a nasty wrenching sound—a wet and sucking sound that's almost impossible to properly describe, and next . . .'"

Molly fell silent then, and the atmosphere in Ricky's living room seemed as heavy as that in the house she was remembering. Finally, Molly sighed:

"And then, Aunt Melda's severed head came bouncing, thumping, and rolling down the stairs," she concluded miserably. "The head was turning end-over-end and leaving splotches of blood on the stairs, seemingly navigating that spiral stairway like a remote-controlled thing. I mean, because there were several places where it could've easily rolled through the stairway railing and dropped down to the floor and yet it didn't do so.

"When Aunt Melda's head finally stopped at the bottom of the stairs, Erin De Mornay walked over and picked it up. Still smiling, Erin turned to me. 'Go,' she told me, pointing at the door. 'You can call the cops whenever you like. I won't be here when they arrive anyway.'

"And then, Erin De Mornay resumed mouthing her cryptic nonsense and, still holding onto Aunt Melda's head, she began climbing that coiling staircase. I fled outside and instantly dialed the cops."

"Wow," said Ricky. "That is one crazy story."

Molly nodded back at him. "Baby, I swear every single word of it is true. And it doesn't even end there. There's more to the story."

"More? After the cops arrived?"

Molly nodded again and then sighed expressively and quite theatrically. "When the cops arrived, they searched the house but of course they didn't find Erin. However, they did find Aunt Melda's remains. But . . . well, even though they found Aunt Melda's head upstairs, she wasn't exactly complete. See, she'd been eaten."

Now, Ricky's eyes bugged out. "Eaten?"

"Yep, large chunks of her body were missing, she had bear-like tooth marks all over her, and both of her thighs had been chewed up like beef jerky. But that's just the tip of the insane iceberg. You recall how I mentioned that the cops didn't find the rotting baby that I'd earlier seen?"

Ricky replied her question with a cautious nod.

"Well," Molly went on, "remember also that I said the walls of that horrible room upstairs were red, like they'd been painted over?" Without waiting for her boyfriend's response, she went on: "Well, Forensics analyzed the red stuff the wall was painted with, and it was human blood." She gave Ricky an eerie smile. "Actually, the blood belonged to a baby who'd gone missing about a fortnight earlier."

"That's just sick," Ricky said glumly.

"And there's two other things."

"There's *more?*"

Molly smiled coldly at him. It wasn't a smile of amusement, but one of resignation to the craziness of the tale she was telling him.

"Yes, because that's why I'm actually telling you all of this now and not at some other time."

"Go on, I'm listening."

"Well, first thing the police did was research the owner of the house. It turned out that the house did belong to Erin De Mornay." Molly wagged a finger at Ricky and then added: "The only problem was that Erin De Mornay had died back in the sixties down south in California."

"What?"

"Yeah, it's true," Molly said. "They showed me photos of her and it was exactly the same woman—in different clothes of course."

"This is insane."

"Oh, it gets even more insane, because Erin De Mornay's fingerprints were all over the house. Back in the fifties she'd been a person of interest in some occult-related murders in Sacramento, so they had her prints on record. So, here in Raynham, MA, sixty years later, we get the bitch's *fresh* fingerprints on the stairway railing, the furniture etc., even on the front door. The cops had no idea what to make of it."

Molly now frowned. "I'm sure you can imagine my frame of mind when I heard all of this. I was already freaking out from what had happened to my aunt, but after the cops told me all of this extra stuff, and I did some internet researching of my own that confirmed the truth of it all, well you can just imagine my mental state. I was two wicker strips short of becoming a basket case."

"I can imagine," Ricky agreed. "I also can't imagine what you were going through."

"So, with Aunt Melda dead, I'm like, out of a job now. So, to pay my house rent and cover my expenses till I found another job, I decided to take up escorting, and Tommy Burke was my first customer."

Ricky began laughing. The laughter bubbled out of him in waves. He let it flow out of him like a river of madness in psycho flood season. Molly watched him with a cool smile on her lips, like she understood exactly what he was going through.

"Sorry 'bout that," Ricky said finally. "I couldn't hold it in."

"I used to laugh like that occasionally too," Molly told him. "Mad laughter was a very effective way to release the insanity I was feeling." Then she wagged a finger at him. "Okay, but I do get the funny part of it. Here I am, just starting sex work after a crazy supernatural experience, and the first guy that hires me just wound up dead . . . in a similarly inexplicable way to my Aunt Melda's passing." Molly now looked very bothered. "And here's the craziest part of this whole thing."

She gave Ricky a searching look. He nodded at her to go on.

"Okay, the spellbook that Erin De Mornay was chanting out of, seems to me to be exactly the same one that our good friend Grady Burke found at the dead man's house. You know—'How to Fucking Succeed in Life?' "

"What?"

"Yes. If it isn't the same book, it's a damn good copy. Same pale-like-pinkish leather, same creepy and cryptic lettering, same nasty and scary ambience."

"But . . ."

Ricky's shocked statement was cut short by the ringing of the doorbell.

"Wonder who that is?" Ricky said, and then got up to go find out.

CHAPTER 40

The person at the front door turned out to be Ricky's landlady, Mrs. Peters.

Mrs. Peters was an elderly woman who lived with her husband in the other half of the duplex. She was tall and angular, with long gray hair and faded blue eyes.

"Oh, good afternoon, Mrs. Peters," Ricky said. Though wondering what could possibly have brought her over to his house today, he was pleased to see her, as her down-to-earth solid presence provided him with an anchor of normal sane reality after the insane story that Molly had just told him.

A story that unfortunately, I believe all the way to the finish line. Molly isn't lying. I can see in her eyes that she isn't. And that means Grady has one hell of a problem on his hands.

"Oh, I'm so glad to catch you at home," the landlady told him with a broad smile. "I saw your car outside, but I couldn't be certain that you were in."

Ricky stepped aside. "Please come in. I'll make us both some coffee."

But instead of doing so, Mrs. Peters shook her head. "Oh no, I don't have the time to stay and chit-chat. There's something important I need to take care of at home."

While Mrs. Peters spoke, Ricky felt there was something strange about her this morning.

Yes, she's her normal pleasant self, but . . . No, there's nothing at all wrong with her—I'm just imagining stuff . . . more mental fallout from Molly's creepy story.

Molly appeared behind Ricky then. "Sweetie, who's at the . . . ? Oh, hello, Mrs. Peters."

"Good afternoon, hon," Mrs. Peters greeted Molly, then she returned her attention to Ricky. "So, like I was just saying, I need to get back to what I was doing, but first there's something I need to give to you."

Ricky nodded. "Yeah, sure, what is it?"

Mrs. Peters held up a small package. "This came in the mail for me yesterday, and I can't make either head or tails of it, or understand who sent it either, nor can Eddie." (Eddie was her husband.) "So I figured I'd give it to you and Molly. You're both youngsters and should relish the challenge of working out the riddle it presents."

While speaking, Mrs. Peters had been pulling a book out of her package.

On seeing the book's pale leather binding and the strange script on its front cover, Ricky Lawson felt faint. Behind him, he heard Molly gasp and he felt glad that she was here with him, as now it was *her* presence and not that of the stolid Mrs. Peters that seemed more of a stable foundation.

"Well, here it is," Mrs. Peters told him and Molly, while handing over the small leather pamphlet. "About the only thing I'm certain of is that it's titled 'How to Succeed in Life.' Tho' how I'm sure of even that, I've no idea, cuz as you'll see for yourselves, it's not even written in English."

"Thanks," Ricky said, feeling horror seep to him from the little volume the moment his fingers touched it. "Molly and I will try to work out what it says."

"Yeah, you both do that. Now, you'll have to excuse me. I need to get back to my Eddie. We've something important to discuss."

"Yeah, sure, Mrs. Peters," Molly said in a small, scared voice.

Smiling and waving back at them both, Mrs. Peters walked brisky down the front porch steps and turned left towards her own half of the duplex.

Ricky watched her go and then stared at Molly.

"What the . . . ?" he said in a shaky voice, holding the copy of 'How to Succeed in Life' up between them. "Baby, what is going on?"

Molly's only reply was a horrified look.

CHAPTER 41

Once, when Gina Luz had told a friend of hers that she felt smothered by Susan Bundy's constant attention, her friend had replied "What do you expect? She's an obese woman; you need to ride her instead of letting her ride you."

Of course, Gina had meant 'smothered' in an emotional sense, but her friend had made a joke out of it.

However, at the moment Gina was putting that advice to good use. She was riding Joe Bundy for all she was worth, like she intended to travel to Texas on his penis.

Joe was obese and extremely hairy; so hairy in fact that Gina felt a little odd herself while riding him, as if he wasn't exactly human, but was rather a giant animated hairball that a cat god had thrown up.

Hairball or not, the sex was satisfying though.

Gina and Joe were in bed now because Susan had called from the Bundy's pizza shop in Fall River to say that she was going shopping.

So, Joe and Gina were using this extension of his sister's absence to cement their new-found lust.

"I know this ain't wise," Joe said as they did it, "but your body's so sweet and I ain't had a woman in ages."

That made Gina grin, and soon they came together.

"Hey, why'd your wife leave you?" Gina asked afterwards, when they were laying side by side with Joe's left arm under her head like a pillow.

Joe grunted. "The normal reasons, meaning of course, that neither of us is really certain why we stopped lovin' one another. We just woke one day and the marriage wasn't workin' anymore." Joe smiled sadly. "Mel got the kids and I got the bills for 'em. I see 'em all once or twice a month when I'm not slaving away cooking Italian pies here."

Gina laughed. "But you're the boss; everyone's at your beck and call, including your sister. And besides, what with your other Bundy's Pizza branches making so much money, you're only keeping this shop going cuz Susan insists that you doing so."

Joe grunted again. Because of his immense bulk this sounded boar-like, or maybe bearlike. "Nah, Susan's got an equal share of everything. She lets me run the biz cuz I'm better than she is with figures, while she's better at recipes and promo and stuff like that. But we sign out everything together, so none of us outspends the other."

"Share and share alike," Gina said. "I like that. You're not screwing her over and vice versa." Then she frowned and raised herself up on an elbow so that she was staring down at him. "Except in this case. Hey, where does that leave li'l ol' me?"

Now, Joe laughed and tweaked Gina's left nipple between a fat finger and a fatter thumb. "Susan ain't gonna appreciate my sharing you with her one bit. I really need to think this through properly."

"Maybe I need to stop working here," Gina suggested. "I can easily break up with Susan that way. Then a few weeks later . . ."

Joe's brow creased up as he thought about it. "Maybe we won't need to do anything so drastic. Just gimme a while to figure this out." He tweaked her nipple again. "But we'll keep your suggestion as our backup plan." He leered at her. "Now come gimme some more sugar!"

"Uh uh, babe," Gina told him, wagging a finger at him. "I'd better get back out front. Your sister didn't travel to Wyoming, she's just down at Cashstretch or the Walmart Supercenter."

"Aw, c'mon," Joe cajoled while grasping at her. "Susan's as fat and out-of-shape as I am. Shopping's gonna take her three hours at least."

But Gina successfully evaded his grasp. She knew it was important to not give him too much of herself yet.

Once Susan is out of the way romantically—damn, is this a messed up love triangle or what?—then I can be more generous to Joe with my body; bang him till he can't see straight, till he's too tired to stand up. But for now . . .

She got off the bed and pulled her clothes back on.

Resigned to the fact that he wouldn't be getting any more sex today, Joe had now hauled himself up to a sitting position and was pouting thoughtfully at Gina.

"You've got a knockout body," he told her.

She liked the sincerity in his voice. "You know, Grady knows about us. He saw me coming out of your office earlier, and even overheard part of our conversation."

Joe mused on that for a few moments, then waved it off. "Ah, Grady's a good kid; minds his own business. He ain't gonna say anything to Susan 'bout us."

Gina frowned. "He might. He's sweet on me."

Joe laughed and pulled himself off the bed. "Well, that's cuz you're so sweet, hon."

Joe walked over to Gina, gave her a kiss and then began sliding his large underpants up his large legs.

"Darling, please have a man-to-man talk with Grady," Gina said. "Explain to him the employment benefits of selective blindness."

Joe laughed and pulled on his XXXL jeans. "Yah, might just do that if . . ." Joe stopped talking. "Hey, what's that book you got with you there?"

Gina shrugged and held out the book to Joe. "It's some weird joke book called 'How to Succeed in Life.' No English words in it whatsoever, but somehow it makes weird sense . . . and it manages to scare the crap out of you on reading it."

Joe took the book from Gina and flipped through it. His smile instantly soured and he looked confused.

"I remember seeing a jokey book when I was younger," Joe said. "Was titled 'Everything that Men know about Women,' but when you opened it up, it was just blank pages."

Gina laughed as she got the joke. "And the joke was on you guys— meaning you know nothing about us ladies, right?"

Joe nodded. "I'm mentioning that cuz this reminds me of that—a name but no content." He handed the book back to Gina. "And while that book was just a harmless war-of-the-sexes joke, this one definitely ain't harmless. I don't know what's written inside of it, but I know I don't like it one bit. You know, you really shouldn't be carrying it around with you. Just touching it feels like bad juju."

Gina gave Joe a perplexed look. "I don't know how, sweetie, but I keep packing it among my stuff." She giggled. "If I were superstitious, I'd say the book was packing *itself* with my stuff."

Joe frowned and pulled his shirt on. "Honey, I am superstitious and I agree that it might be doing that."

Gina laughed. "Oh c'mon, don't be silly."

Joe opened his mouth to reply her, but before he could do so, the door to his bedroom swung open and Susan was standing framed in the doorway.

CHAPTER 42

Susan was holding a taser in one hand and a large meat cleaver in the other. She looked angrily from her brother to her girlfriend.

"I knew something was going on between the both of you," she said and waved the taser at them. "And so I only pretended to go shopping today after leaving Fall River."

"It's not what it looks like," Joe said with a stupid look on his face.

"We're all in your bedroom, Gina is only half dressed, and your pants are open, dumbass," Susan retorted. "What else could it be?"

And on that statement, she aimed the taser at Joe and fired. Joe hadn't yet done up the buttons of his shirt. The taser barbs hit him in his hairy chest and he in turn hit the floor, where he lay trembling.

Once Joe was out of commission for the moment, Susan dropped the taser on the bed and advanced on Gina, waving the meat cleaver menacingly at her. "And as for you, you heartbreaker . . ."

"Please, darling, don't do anything rash!" Gina pleaded, with her eyes not leaving the massive cleaver Susan was holding for a second. "Joe forced himself on me! Honest!"

Susan smiled coldly. "Yes, I know he did. He's forceful like that. It's an asset in business, but not in relationships."

Gina backed away from Susan, trying to escape around her big body.

Then Susan swung the cleaver.

Gina tried to duck out of the way, but only now did she realize that she'd unwittingly backed herself into a corner.

She had no escape.

Swung with all the force of Susan's jealousy, the cleaver hit Gina flush in the face and went deep into her head.

Susan let go of the cleaver handle. Gina remained on her feet, staggering around, while blood squirted between the cleaver blade and her flesh. The blade had missed partitioning Gina's nose, but both her upper and lower lips were sliced in half, and with the way the huge blade was stuck into her lower jaw, her mouth was locked in a half-open position.

She jerked about like a puppet; dead on her feet, but with her body not yet having come to terms with the new order of things.

Knowing that Gina was done for, Susan left her alone for the moment.

She returned her attention to her brother, who was just coming out of his tremors. His tased predicament probably exacerbated by the family obesity, Joe was flopping about and trying to regain control of his limbs. Even to Susan, who shared the family obesity, Joe looked comical.

While wishing she had a multi-shot police taser instead of these one-shot civvie ones, so that she could gift Joe another jolt of its electric sting, Susan instead picked up a heavy Native American statuette from her brother's bedroom table and knocked him out with it.

Before Susan hit him, Joe had made it up to his knees, but now his eyes rolled up back into his head and he flopped down to the floor again.

Susan then rolled him over onto his back. Joe's head was bleeding somewhere above the hairline now, but Susan figured it served the sonofabitch right.

She heard the 'thump' behind her that announced Gina's similar collapse to the floor and smiled in cruel satisfaction.

Then, Susan quickly pulled out a roll of duct tape from her handbag and taped Joe's hands together behind his back. Then, after similarly securing Joe's ankles and taping over his mouth so that he couldn't yell for help when he properly revived, she returned her attention to Gina again.

"Damn, are you one messy bitch," Susan whispered in complete disgust when she saw the mess that her cheating girlfriend had made of her brother's bedroom.

With her brain still refusing to give up the fight for life, Gina was now back up on her knees and was attempting to pull the cleaver blade out of her head. But, either because she was too weakened by blood loss to get a firm grip on the cleaver handle, or because attempting to move it agitated the nerves in her head and filled her with pain, or because the cleaver blade had damaged her brain too badly for her to complete what she was doing, for one reason or the other, Gina kept on grasping the cleaver handle and then letting go of it again, while more and more blood spilled out of her face.

Or maybe the simple fear of bleeding to death was her problem.

Whatever her reason was, however, Gina's constant motion and left-right swivels had coated the bedroom rug, the furniture, and the clothes in Joe's closet with blood. Looking at the room gave Susan the impression that someone had exploded a human firework in here—one that was filled with blood and meat, and that red liquid streamers had squirted out all over the place and afterwards refused to disperse.

Susan watched Gina stumble around aimlessly for a while.

Joe had meanwhile revived again, and was rolling on the floor, turning himself over onto his back so he could see what was happening in the room.

Susan let her brother turn himself over. He wasn't about going anywhere.

She also wasn't worried about anyone coming in and seeing what she'd just done.

Her first action on returning from the town of Fall River had been to give everyone the day off and then put up the 'WE'RE CLOSED' sign. It was only after both Grady Burke and Katie Jensen had left the shop premises that she'd headed in back to surprise these two cheaters.

Susan finally tired of watching Gina ramble and jerk about. With a smile on her face, she walked over to her.

"Here, sweetie, let me help you with that," she told Gina and then yanked the cleaver blade out of her head.

"Th-th-th-th-thanks!" Gina mumbled as blood now really began squirting from her head.

"Don't mention it, what else are lovers for?" Susan told Gina, and then, swinging the cleaver sideways, she hacked Gina's head right off of her neck with a single brutal swipe.

Then, while Joe stared at her in horror and tried desperately to free himself, Susan knelt down beside Gina's fallen body and began chopping her up into pieces, quickly separating her into arms, legs, and miscellaneous portions of anatomy.

And once that was done and her erstwhile girlfriend was nothing more than a butchered mess spread across her brother's bedroom, she got out her copy of 'How to Succeed in Life' from her handbag and flipped through it.

"Alright, that's the first part of the ritual completed," she nodded to herself after a while. Then she gestured down at her brother. "The next part of how *I'll* succeed in life concerns you, you POS!"

She laughed when Joe understandably pissed his pants.

CHAPTER 43

Today had already struck Grady as being a supremely weird one. Odd from hour six a.m.

First off, he'd gotten a weird vibe at home before leaving. And that weird vibe had later seemed to transmit itself to the pizza shop.

Or maybe I carried it along with me from home.

Oddest of all had been Susan's abrupt return from Fall River and her dismissal of all staff for the day.

Okay, so I get that it's not like we have anything to do today now that Joe blocked the gas valves to the ovens or whatever it was that he did to get Susan out of the shop; so sending us home is logical enough. But . . . does Susan suspect Joe and Gina are bumping bodies? After some more consideration, the question made him laugh. *But even if she does suspect something's going on, what's she gonna do? Cook and eat them both?*

Grady drove on homeward.

Okay, so now I've unexpectedly got Sunday afternoon off. So what am I gonna do with myself today? Ricky's got an afternoon shift today and he'll be leaving for work soon, so hanging out with him is out. I'll just head home and watch some stuff on . . . oh no!

Grady's lips got a sour twist to them as he recalled that today was Kayla's epic tranny sendoff orgy.

Hell no, I'm not going home to listen to that!

Realizing that if his older sister knew he was in the house, she might even enlist his help as a cameraman if she was short of hands, Grady resolved not to return home till early evening. Even riding the Viagra train, there was only so long that Kayla and her kinky friends could screw for.

Then he saw that he was approaching a strip of restaurants and grocery stores and the sight of them reminded him he'd not yet eaten today.

Lunch is a good way to use up a few minutes.

He drove into the parking lot of the nearest restaurant and killed the car engine.

As Grady was exiting his Toyota Camry, it suddenly occurred to him that he was forgetting something, so he turned and looked back into the car.

And then he frowned.

Oh shit, the book from the pit. Never leave home without it.

He leaned over to the front passenger seat and picked up the copy of 'How to Succeed in Life' that lay there. Of course, Grady didn't recall putting the leather book in his vehicle, or even taking it out of the house with him this morning, but he figured that he must have done so.

Or else it won't be here now, would it?

Actually, Grady could've sworn that until he'd thought he was missing something, the damn book hadn't even been there on the front passenger seat.

But of course, that was crazy reasoning, and Grady didn't like to think that he was hallucinating. For the first day since his father's death, he'd managed not to vape up this morning before leaving home and he didn't want to start any thoughts running in his head that might make him need cannabis assistance today also.

He straightened up again, slipped the book into his pocket, and then locked the car door.

The book's unexpected presence here was just another cog in the today's gears of strange.

And besides, Grady thought as he walked into the restaurant to order some breakfast, *the book actually gives me something to do today. Today and possibly tomorrow too, I've all the time in the world to try to read it and make sense of it.*

CHAPTER 44

"I can't get over how impossibly creepy this is," Ricky told Molly. "You're just getting through telling me about how you think this same book had something to do with your aunt's death, and here we get a copy delivered to us."

They were seated on the living room couch again, with the book between them.

"Maybe we're supposed to read it," Molly said.

She moved to pick the book up, but before she could do so, Ricky covered the little volume with his right hand and shook his head at her. Then he pointed to his thigh, where the wounds her fingernails had made had now become a quintet of scars. "Baby, don't. Remember what happened the last time."

Molly nodded but looked frustrated. "Yeah, okay. But aren't you at least curious as to why we're getting a copy of it like this?"

"After what you earlier told me about your Aunt Melda's exit from life, I'm wary about being curious." He took his hand off of the book's cover. "Just touching it gives me enough of the creeps."

"I agree. But we can't just leave it here."

"Maybe we should give it to Grady," Ricky said. "The copy he found doesn't seem to have harmed him so far."

"You're forgetting what happened to his dad."

"Yeah," Ricky slowly agreed, "but that's—"

And then a loud howl silenced him.

The unexpected noise from outside the house shattered the suburban weekend peace.

Ricky and Molly stared at one another in shocked silence, until Molly found her voice and asked: "What was that?"

Ricky gaped back at her. "Sounded like it came from Mrs. Peters' house."

And then the howl came again. This time Ricky and Molly understood that the noise wasn't really that loud, but because they were both already on edge due to the creepy book that was there on the couch with them, the moaning—like the grunting of a dying bull—resounded like the tolling of a doomsday bell in their troubled minds.

"Yeah, it is coming from Mr. and Mrs. Peters' place!" Ricky said when the howling came again. He gave Molly a worried look and extended a hand to pull her up from the couch. "Come on, we'd better go see what's wrong. It sounds like Mr. Peters has hurt himself badly!"

So, Ricky and Molly left their own half of the duplex building and ran next door.

Reinforcing the impression that the intensity of the agonized sound they were hearing was mostly in their bothered minds, the street on which their house stood was its regular unperturbed Sunday afternoon self, with no one showing the same curiosity that they were.

Nonetheless, the agonized howling came again just as they reached the Peters' front door, which was flung wide open as if husband and wife had just admitted a crowd into their home.

Ricky and Molly ran inside and then, once they were inside the Peters' living room, both skidded to a halt and gaped.

"Wh-wha . . . ?" was all that either Ricky or Molly could mouth in disbelief.

What they were staring at had them both struck speechless. Molly instantly gave a howl of her own and gripped Ricky tight.

Yes, Mr. Peters *was* the one howling in pain. But the problem was that Mr. Peters was VERY dead. Mr. Peters' severed head sat on his couch, where it was wedged upright in the couch's left angle, while his headless corpse lay belly-down over the coffee table, with the position of his body suggesting that he'd been arranged that way so he could be decapitated using the bloody axe on the floor by his feet.

And yet, watched by both Ricky and Molly, Mr. Peters' decapitated head opened its mouth and let out a low howl of pain, after which it seemed to say something else, but in this case the words had no volume at all.

"Where's Mrs. Peters?" Molly asked in fright. "We'd better check if she's still alive."

"Uh uh, baby. Let's get out of here and call the po—"

Ricky's reply was truncated by Mrs. Peters' voice saying: "Oh calm down, Eddie. Yes, I know it's hot down there, but then you wanted us to go somewhere warm for our next vacation."

Startled by the landlady's voice, but relieved that she was alive, Ricky and Molly turned to look at her.

"Mrs. Peters?" Ricky whispered. "What happened in here? Who killed your husband?"

But she didn't look at him. Ricky's attempt to go to the old woman was halted by Molly, who held on tight to him.

"Look at her bloody hands," Molly whispered. "*She's* the one who killed him. And now she's holding two knives."

Mrs. Peters still gave no sign of noticing either her young tenant or his girlfriend. Her entire focus was on the moaning severed head on the couch.

Once again the head groaned and this time rolled its eyes like it was in hellish pain.

Mrs. Peters put her knives down on the coffee table, and then she sat down beside the severed head and patted its hair comfortingly.

"It's okay, Eddie, I'll be with you soon," she told the head.

Her short speech seemed to calm the head because it stopped moaning. Smiling with pleasure, Mrs. Peters now retrieved the two knives that she'd earlier placed on the coffee table.

"Okay, Eddie, here I come to join you," the old lady said, and then she crossed her hands and placed one knife against each side of her throat, with their cutting edges pressed hard into her skin to that blood dribbled along their blades.

And crazily, now her husband's severed head sounded like it was moaning encouragement to her.

"No, Mrs. Peters, don't you do that!" Ricky shouted.

He tried to move then, to stop Mrs. Peters from killing herself. But even though now Molly let go of him, his legs felt encased in leaden boots that reached up to his thighs.

He was still attempting to take his third step across the room when Mrs. Peters dragged both knife blades violently across her throat.

Mrs. Peters' neck slit open as cleanly as if it was beef being prepared for barbeque. And then, with her spine now visible as a white bone column in the depths of her neck, the arterial spray of blood began, bright gushing crimson, and with its first jets traveling so far across the living room that Molly and Ricky (who'd regained proper control of his legs once his landlady had successfully slit her throat open) were both forced to get out of its way to avoid being drenched in the red liquid.

As she committed suicide, Mrs. Peters had been smiling. But all of a sudden her expression turned to one of immense tragedy and then she slumped back dead.

Her husband's head stopped moaning then and apparently died for good too.

"I'm getting out of here!" Molly shrieked and ran out of the house.

Fighting the urge to throw up, Ricky got out his cellphone and called the police.

And for certain, I'm not gonna tell the cops any of that stuff about the severed head talking, he thought while the phone connected to the 9-1-1 operator. *Grady is the only person who's gonna believe what we just saw.*

"Hello. 9-1-1, what is your emergency?"

"I'd like to report a murder-suicide . . ."

Ricky gave the woman on the phone the details of what had just happened. And then he made a video of the dead couple to show to Grady.

And then Ricky Lawson went outside to comfort Molly.

CHAPTER 45

After Grady drove off to Bundy's Pizza place that Sunday noon, Kayla held her Butthole Bash Orgy as scheduled.

In anticipation of her grand sendoff from the porno biz, Kayla had spent most of yesterday getting things ready. To this end, now she had three video cameras set up on tripods in her bedroom, with a further one in her en suite bathroom, ready for the grand finale of her show, when all of the participants would urinate on her head, as a sort of 'golden blessing' for her life after porn.

The other five participants in the Butthole Bash Orgy arrived on schedule, with Mr. And Mrs. Stainless Strange arriving in their usual latex clothing. Along with them, they'd brought another of their kinky kind, this person a young male gimp named Bubbles, who had his penis locked in a metal cock cage.

The other two participants were both transgender women, a blonde named Destiny Cable and a black woman named Shannon Banxxx.

Except for Bubbles the gimp, everyone else had been present at Tommy Burke's funeral service two days earlier. (The Stainless Stranges had told Kayla they'd been present at the funeral and had confirmed this by describing some of the other attendees who'd been at the funeral home, but Kayla still didn't know what they looked like beneath their latex masks because they'd not come over afterwards to offer their condolences.)

Everyone was raring to go, with their rectums all enemaed nice and clean. There were tubes of lube everywhere and also strips of condoms for Destiny Cable, who alone of them all wasn't on PrEP medication.

"Okay, freaks," Shannon told everyone at the start of the sex show, "I need y'all to remember one thing—whoever ain't either fucking someone or being fucked by someone should film everyone else with their cellphone cameras. HD or 4K resolution if you got that."

"If you can film *while* you're being fucked, that's a plus," Mrs. Strange added with a giggle.

The show began, with everyone—the four trans women and two men—having sex in all sort of kinds of combinations. Various sex toys were unpacked, used and abused, and then discarded. Everyone present got sodomized at least two or three times.

Seeing as this was Kayla's farewell bash, the focus of the orgy constantly shifted from her to the other women and the men and then unfailingly back to her again.

Most of the time either Mrs. Stainless Strange or Shannon Banxxx was directing proceedings.

After Mrs. Strange creampied the gimp and pulled out of him, the gimp farted twice in quick succession.

Kayla laughed loudly. "Hey, stop playing jazz with your ass!" she told the gimp.

Kayla was having great fun. Today she was quite high on cannabis and her world was all jasmine-scented rainbows.

Yep, this is exactly how I want my porno farewell to be! she thought enthusiastically.

At this point Kayla and Mrs. Stainless Strange were tag-teaming Bubbles the gimp on the bed. Mrs. Strange was in the gimp's butt, and he was sucking Kayla off.

And then suddenly, Kayla felt Bubbles tapping her on the thigh.

At this time, she was holding his head firmly, forcing his mouth down on her cock to gag him, and as such his lips were right down at the root of her penis, pressed firmly into her pubic hair.

When Bubbles began tapping on Kayla's leg, she at first thought she was in too deep in his throat and he wanted to pull back so he could breathe in a little air. Mrs. Strange was meanwhile thrusting into Bubbles' backside with abandon.

Kayla let go of Bubbles' head. But then she realized that Bubbles seemed unable to pull his mouth off of her.

The gimp was tapping away at her thighs with some urgency now, and yet his plight amused Kayla.

Oops, I've heard of people getting glued together during sexual intercourse, but this has to be a first. Particularly since I'm not exactly hung like Kong.

With Mrs. Strange still sodomizing the gimp and completely unaware of the young man's troubles, Kayla began trying to separate herself from Bubbles.

And now, to her surprise, she discovered that she couldn't do so. When she pulled her body away from Bubbles, his head came along with her crotch as if glued to it. And she could feel that his jaw was slack down there, it wasn't like his teeth were holding onto her erection.

Oh, my dear God, what is happening here?

By now, Bubbles had stopped thumping on her and was going limp, his arms losing their ability to hold his torso upright, so that now he was held in place solely by his head.

Mrs. Strange now noticed that there was a problem, but she simply assumed she was going in too deep in the young man's ass and began holding back with her thrusts.

Still confused, Kayla looked first left and then right. Destiny Cable, the blond girl, was giving a blowjob to Mr. Stainless Strange, while Shannon filmed them with her cellphone. Destiny took her mouth off of Mr. Strange's cock, sucked in some vape smoke, and then ducked her lips down on him again.

Apparently, no one except Kayla realized they had a big problem in here.

"For God's sake, somebody do something, he's choking to death on my dick!" Kayla yelled as Bubbles now began spasming.

That got everyone's attention, and now they all stopped having sex and turned their attention to Kayla and Bubbles.

Once he'd sized up the nature of the crisis, Mr. Strange instantly took hold of the gimp's shoulders and jerked him backward. But that didn't work either. Sure, Bubbles went backward, but Kayla went along with him. Kayla just managed to keep from falling right on top of Bubbles and possibly breaking both his neck and her penis (because owning to the wonders of Viagra, she was still bone-hard inside of the distressed young man's head).

And then, to everyone's horror, bright red blood began streaming from Bubbles' nostrils.

"Shit, he's dying!" someone whispered in a frightened voice. "We'd better dial 9-1-1 fast!"

"I'll do it! I'll do it!" Shannon yelped and hurried over to get her cellphone from the table where everyone had left their phones.

While Shannon dialed for an ambulance, blood kept streaming from Bubbles' nostrils, while he flapped about like a landed fish.

Kayla was horrified. Most of the blood that the gimp was ejecting from his nostrils was landing in her pubic hair and dribbling down her thighs.

I've gotta get out of this connection to him! I gotta do it!

With that desperate thought in mind, Kayla once more braced her hands against Bubbles' shoulders, shoved them forward, and at the same time gave a mighty backward wrench of her hips.

This time she instantly felt herself pluck free of Bubbles' mouth.

Her motion was however ill-timed.

Right at the moment when Kayla got free of Bubbles, was when Shannon Banxxx, who'd been looking away from everyone while calling 9-1-1, turned around and faced the others in the room.

"An ambulance is on the way!" Shannon told them all.

But while speaking, Shannon Banxxx was walking towards the bed, while Kayla, propelled by her intense revulsion for what had just happened, was coming off of the bed, still powered by the force that had unstuck Bubbles from her crotch.

With Shannon fast approaching the bed at an angle, and Kayla backing off of it, the pair collided, with the result that Kayla was knocked back forward onto the bed, but Shannon was knocked sideways and into the front bedroom window.

The window drapes were open, to permit light into the bedroom, but the window itself was shut.

No one thought that Kayla had hit Shannon that hard, but apparently she had, because Shannon crashed into the window with such force that she shattered the window and went partly through it. The impact knocked out half of the glass in the window and left Shannon lying with her head outside in the air and her neck on the window frame.

"Guys, I think Bubbles is dead," Mr. Strange was saying right when Shannon hit the glass. "I think he's dead!"

And thereafter, the group in the bedroom was divided in two. While Kayla and Destiny Cable stayed with Bubbles' corpse, Mr. and Mrs. Stainless Strange hurried over to the window to see what was up with Shannon Banxxx, who'd not so much as twitched a muscle since she'd hit the window.

Shannon stood bent over there, braced up against the window frame, with her hands on the ledge and her butt up in the air like she was awaiting a dick in her ass. Thanks to the boner pills that they'd all taken, her own penis was still hard.

"I didn't think she hit the window hard enough to put out her lights," Mrs. Strange whispered to her husband.

"I didn't think she hit it hard enough to break the glass," he whispered back to her.

"I hope she's not dead also," Kayla groaned. "Oh my God, this is a nightmare!"

"Oh, the slut's fine," Mr. Strange told everyone after leaning out of the window and examining the black transwoman's neck and confirming that she hadn't stabbed her throat on any glass shards. "I'll just carefully lift her back inside and . . ."

"Shit! Look out!" Mrs. Strange yelled then and grabbed her husband by the shoulders and pulled him backward.

She'd screamed so loudly that even Kayla and Destiny, who'd resumed trying to bring back Bubbles from the dead, turned to stare at the window again.

They saw what was going to happen, fractions of a second before it did.

Mrs. Strange had screamed because she'd noticed that the upper half of the glass window was dropping, sliding down inside of the window frame. (Shannon Banxxx's crash into the window had somehow shattered and knocked all of the lower half of the glass pane out of place, but left the upper half of it intact.)

The loose upper glass slid down like a guillotine.

Unfortunately for unconscious Shannon Banxxx, Mrs. Strange had grabbed her husband before he'd gotten a firm grip on Shannon's shoulders. This resulted in Mr. Strange letting go of Shannon, instead of pulling her also to safety when he fell back into the room.

With Mr. Strange now safely out of its way, the descending glass pane cut off Shannon Banxxx's head as cleanly as if she'd been Marie Antoinette during the French revolution. Her hands, both of which had also been up on the window ledge, also went the way of her head.

Kayla took one look at Shannon's headless body squirting blood out of her bedroom window and fainted outright. She collapsed on top of Bubbles' corpse.

The ambulance that Shannon Banxxx had phoned for arrived about a minute later, and the paramedics were ironically greeted by her severed head waiting for them near the front door of the Burke's house.

They later found her severed hands amidst the lawn grass.

CHAPTER 46

In the living apartments that comprised the rear of the Bundy's Pizzas building, Susan Bundy was meanwhile going ahead with her plans to become a success in life.

At the moment, she was sitting opposite her brother, whom she'd leveraged up so that he was sitting against the foot of his bed.

Susan was drenched crimson now, her clothes soaked through with Gina's blood.

"You shouldn't have stolen Gina from me, Joe," Susan said. "You know how few girlfriends I have." Then she laughed at him and waved her copy of 'How to Succeed in Life' at him. "But that doesn't matter now. Once I complete the ritual in this book, I'll be rich and famous enough to have any woman I want, even Ellen DeGeneres or presidents' wives if I want them."

Joe couldn't reply to this as his mouth was still duct-taped over. Susan's eyes had a little madness in them now, and Joe's did also. But while in Susan's case, she appeared to have snapped and completely lost it, Joe was simply going out of his mind from fright caused by seeing what Susan had just done to Gina, who now lay scattered around the bedroom in what Joe suddenly realized wasn't the random dispersal it at first seemed to be, but was actually a geometric figure that wasn't exactly a pentagram but was close enough. Viewed from the correct insane POV, each of Gina's severed limbs formed one tip of a five-pointed star, with her head marking its fifth projection, and with the lined-up arrangement of her guts, lungs, and other internal organs filling/tracing out the other connections.

Gina's heart lay right in the middle of the human mess.

Susan said, "Okay, now let's get this over with," and picked up the cleaver she'd killed Gina with. She frowned coldly at her brother. "Sorry, Joe, but you can't make an omelet without . . . no, let me bring that a little closer to home, Joe—you can't make good pizza without cheese . . . or in this case, succeed in life without cutting out some human hearts." She gestured around the room at Gina's remains. "Sorry, Joe, I'm not going to do you like I did her, but I do need your

137

heart to complete the ritual. So, it's goodbye, brother, and thank you for stealing my girlfriend. I couldn't ever have gone through with this otherwise."

Joe began squirming about like crazy, but just like with Gina, there was no escape for him. Susan surged forward like an ocean wave and slammed the cleaver into the side of his neck, where it sank in very deep.

(Susan had actually intended to behead Joe like she'd done to Gina, but Joe's neck was twice as thick as Gina's.)

Then Susan jerked the cleaver out again and watched Joe squirt blood into the air and jerk about and gurgle and die, while his eyes rolled crazily in their sockets.

When Joe finally fell sideways with a soft thump, Susan smiled to herself.

The bedroom rug squelched like a swamp now beneath her feet, soft and mushy with blood.

"Everything's almost ready now," she whispered to herself. "Now I need to cut his heart out."

Being an expert cook, it didn't take Susan long at all to extract Joe's heart from his chest. And then she placed the severed heart in the middle of her occultic rearrangement of Gina's deconstructed corpse, beside Gina's own heart.

Finally, because he was too large for her to either carry or drag him, Susan rolled Joe's body next to the two hearts. Doing this made an additional mess because when Susan had cut Joe open to extract his heart, his intestines had spilled out of his belly.

Then, after taking a short breather, she picked up the demonic self-help book and searched through its pages for the spell she needed to cast.

Susan had discovered that the further you read into the book, the longer you spent studying it, the easier it became to understand its indecipherable script. At first she'd needed close to a minute before the nonsense writing made sense to her. Now, however, it took mere seconds before she'd found her place in the book and began pronouncing the ritual spell.

Standing outside of the flesh-and-blood pentagram that she'd created from Gina's remains, Susan chanted away.

She wasn't exactly certain of what she was saying, and at a point it even seemed to her that the book had taken control of her tongue and was reciting itself through her lips.

And then, once she'd completed the spell, Susan Bundy smiled in awed fascination as the dismantled arms and legs of her murdered girlfriend began dragging themselves across the floor to the middle of the geometric pattern that had been formed from her flesh, aiming themselves at where the pair of removed human hearts were.

CHAPTER 47

"Wow!" Grady told Ricky the next morning, while the two of them were seated in his house for a crucial powwow. "It's like they say: bad stuff don't just rain on you; it pours. What we're experiencing here is a hailstorm of bad stuff."

Ricky nodded soberly. "Tell me about it. How's Kayla doing now?"

Grady gestured upstairs. "Sedated in her bedroom. She's understandably devastated by all that happened. She's additionally mortified that, because of the wonders of modern tech, sooner or later, everyone on the planet will get to watch what happened yesterday."

Ricky nodded. "I believe you. I saw the video." Ricky frowned. "What happened to Mrs. Peters and old Eddie was just as bad, maybe even worse. Man, I kept dreaming of her cutting her throat open all night."

Ricky had shown the video he'd made of the old couple to Grady, and vice versa, Grady too had shown him some videos from Kayla's cellphone.

"I'm very glad Kayla and her porn star friends were filming everything," Grady said. "Or else, my sis would now be looking a really long stretch of prison time. Were it not for those videos, the police might just have assumed the lot of them set out to make a snuff film in the first place."

This was quite true.

Everything that had happened in Kayla's bedroom yesterday afternoon had been captured on camera, and as such the police investigation was over almost before it began.

According to the coroner, Bubbles' throat had simply constricted around the head of Kayla's penis during deepthroat and refused to loosen up. And then he'd suffered a fatal brain hemorrhage.

And as for poor Shannon Banxxx, in her case it was even more obvious what had happened.

Just a terrible, terrible accident.

***

On waking up this morning, Grady (who was originally scheduled to work the early/afternoon shift today) had phoned the pizza shop to ask if work would be resuming today.

He'd gotten no reply, so then he'd called Joe's, Susan's, and finally Gina's personal numbers. No reply either.

Finally, not wanting to drive downtown for nothing and leave Kayla all alone at home, Grady had called both Katie Jensen, who'd been (wo)manning the shop counter yesterday, and Jimmy Hutch, one of the other pizza delivery guys whom he knew also had the earlier shift today.

Katie and Jimmy had both told him they'd call and let him know what was happening today once they arrived at the pizzeria, but so far he'd not heard back from either of them.

***

"It blows tho'," Grady complained to Ricky. "This house will soon be called the Weirdo's Kinky House of Death."

"Yeah, but you've got some money now. So just buy another place and move." Ricky looked glum. "Unlike myself, who has to keep living next to my House of Death."

"Dude, what was that like?"

"Same as here, I guess. Cops everywhere asking a billion questions that Molly and I had no answers to." He frowned. "Unlike your place, the other side of our duplex is now an advert for yellow and black tape."

Grady grimaced. "This blows, bro. Hey, where's Molly? Why didn't you bring her with you? I'd've thought she'd be too creeped out to stay home alone."

"She's more scared of what Kayla might do on seeing her than of any ghosts."

Grady frowned. "Aw, c'mon, dude, after yesterday's experience? Even Kayla knows now that Molly didn't kill pops."

Ricky nodded to that. "Yeah, true. And there's something else . . ." Ricky pulled his copy of 'How to Succeed in Life' out of his pocket and dropped it on the coffee table. "Molly is staying home to research on this thing."

Grady sighed now and pulled his own copy out of a pants pocket and laid it beside Ricky's. "Somehow, I wasn't surprised to hear that you guys also have one now. Of course, the big question is 'why?'"

"That's precisely what Molly is attempting to find out," Ricky said with an agreeing nod. "I left her to it to do because of her background working with her psychic aunt."

"Why don't we simply ask Molly's aunt for help?"

"She's dead." Ricky now spent ten or so minutes explaining in macabre detail to Grady how Melda Woods had lost her head.

"I don't wanna say that we're magically fucked here," Grady said afterwards, "but it's definitely starting to look that way."

The two of them looked at the identical creepy books on the table, like they were twin evil eyes staring out of some impossible place, or . . . twin windows into hell.

"Five people dead so far," Ricky said. "And that's not counting the dead guy in whose house you found the damned thing. Maybe we should just read it through to the end and see what it's all about anyway."

Grady laughed. "Yeah, right. I tried that yesterday, most likely at the same time that your landlady was killing her husband and herself and Kayla was deepthroating that guy to death."

"And?" Ricky asked. "What did you find out? Molly and I had originally discussed reading through the book also, but after what happened to Mr. and Mrs. Peters neither of us had the stomach for it."

While saying this, Ricky unconsciously scratched the fingernail scars on his thigh.

"Well, it's the same thing as before," Grady said, gesturing at the books. "It obviously isn't in any earthly language, but I—of course, by 'I' I mean all of us—can understand exactly what is written inside the book if I concentrate long and hard enough. And the time required to gain that interpretation of its contents seems to shorten after a while."

Grady frowned. "Okay, take yesterday as a case in point. I found that I can read the book for as long as I want to, but immediately I close it, sometimes even if I get distracted by something while reading and I look away for too long, I instantly forget what I've read. I'm left with nothing except a nauseating dread of having learnt secrets better left unknown." Grady shuddered, but was completely unaware of doing so. "And meanwhile," he went on, "I'm extremely aware that if

I keep reading the book, if I persevere with studying its forbidden content, I will soon reach a point in the narrative at which memory will be granted me, but with awful consequences."

He now looked searchingly at Ricky to see what he thought.

"Same vibe here," Ricky agreed. "That day when Molly and I read it together, we both understood it, but afterwards all I could remember is that what I just read in the book scared me shitless. And craziest of all might be that the book seemed to approve of our reading it."

"Yeah, I noticed that too, that the book seemed to have some kind of demonic intelligence behind it that approved of my studying it."

They both mused on that in silence for a while. Then a thought clearly occurred to Ricky, because he scratched in his hair for a few seconds and then asked: "Dude, I'm really worried. How many copies of this book are there exactly?"

Grady looked at him for a few moments, then seemed to get the point of the question. "Good question. I have one, you have one, Kayla has one—"

"She does?"

"She does."

"How . . . ?"

"She said I actually brought two copies of the book home with me that night, not one." He shrugged at the confused look on Ricky's face. "Yep, dude, go figure."

"You know, this stuff has got my head spinning. I almost could do with some cannabis vape right now."

Grady shook his head firmly at Ricky. "Later, dude. Let's work this out with clear heads." He resumed speaking, now counting on his fingers. "Okay, so I've got one, you've got one," he glanced upstairs, "sis has got one, and Gina's got one. That about sums it up."

"Wait, Gina's got one of these too? How . . . ?"

"Yep. I saw it in her skirt pocket after she got through banging the boss."

Now Ricky smiled. "Banging the boss? I thought she was dating Susan."

"At the moment she's dating both of them."

"And yourself?"

"No sympathy sex anywhere on my horizon unfortunately. She told me so herself. I need to go start my own pizza franchise to get laid by the pretty girls."

Ricky shook his head as if to clear it. "Sorry, I'm getting distracted. But, how the hell did Gina get a copy of 'How to Succeed in Life?' "

Grady wagged a finger in the air. "And even more important—*why* did *she* receive a copy of the book?"

He leaned forward and tapped both volumes on the coffee table. "We're all getting copies of this piece of shit for a reason. And whoever is sending them to us is playing for keeps."

"No doubt about that," Ricky agreed. "Dude, I'm worried. I don't wanna wind up headless or eaten by my own guts and neither do you. How long before the Reaper comes calling for us too?"

Now Grady's face reflected Ricky's worries. "Hopefully not before we figure out what this is all about and save our asses. But we're gonna need . . ."

Then Grady paused. First he looked at the clock on the wall, then he looked at the time on his wristwatch, and then he just looked confused.

"What's the matter?" Ricky prompted.

"This is odd," Grady slowly replied. "This is very odd. Disturbingly odd."

"What is?" Ricky asked.

"Remember I told you how we didn't open the pizza shop yesterday?"

Ricky scratched his thigh and frowned. "Yeah, you started off telling me 'bout how Joe had something to do with that, but you didn't properly explain cuz then we switched to talking 'bout Kayla."

"Grady nodded. "Listen, before you came over, I called the shop to ask about work today and got no reply. Not from Joe, not from Susan, and not from Gina either. So then I called both Katie and Jimmy and asked them to call me when they arrived for the early shift and let me know what's happening, so that I don't leave Kayla all alone here and drive over there for nothing."

"And . . . ?"

"And it's been two full hours now since the pizza shop would've opened and I haven't yet heard back from either Katie or Jimmy." He frowned at his bestie. "Do you understand what I'm thinking here . . . particularly after I just told you that Gina also has a copy of these damn books with her?"

"Oh shit!" Ricky said. "Not Gina too. Dude, call the shop again. Call everyone again."

So, Grady called. First he called the pizza shop's two landlines, and then he called Joe's and Susan's and Gina's and Katie's and Jimmy's personal numbers. All with no reply.

Finally he hung up and stared at Ricky in horror.

"I think we'd better get our asses over there like they're on fire," Ricky told him.

Grady nodded, then he frowned and pointed upstairs. "Sis?"

Ricky shook his head. "Our evil book has already had its fun with her. I think Kayla is safe now. I think the book has shifted its theater of horror to your workplace."

Grady nodded. He grabbed his car keys from the coffee table and then he and Ricky hurriedly left the house.

"Hey, we forgot to bring the books along," Ricky pointed out as they piled into the front of Grady's black Camry. "What if we need them for something?"

Grady laughed coldly and turned the key in the ignition. "Dude, you really don't know what we're dealing with here. Look in the backseat, or in the glove compartment. Try the backseat first."

"Huh?" But Ricky did as he was told, turning to peer back between the seats.

A moment later he stared at Grady in horrified amazement. "What the . . . how did they get in your ride?"

Grady laughed again. "Don't sweat it, bro. I don't understand it either. But rest assured that, wherever we go, those books are gonna tag along too. They're like having your psycho ex stalking you."

Grady backed the vehicle out of his driveway and headed for work.

CHAPTER 48

"This is odd," Grady told Ricky as they drove into the Bundy's Pizzas parking lot.

"What do you mean?"

With both hands busy on the steering wheel, Grady nodded towards the vehicles already in the parking lot. "Everyone's cars are here. That's Joe and Susan's pickup truck, and that's Gina's red Subaru. And that's Jimmy's ride over there. Katie normally gets a ride in from her husband."

"O-o-kay . . . Meaning that everyone should be present here this afternoon, and yet *no one* is answering their phones," Ricky worked out aloud while Grady maneuvered his car to a parking space to the left of the shop's front entrance.

From where he'd parked, Grady and Ricky could both see the full extent of the front room through the shopfront windows, with the restaurant area on their left and the customer service counter on their right. The shop interior was completely deserted, although it did look like Katie's handbag was up on the service counter.

"Seems like there's no one inside," Grady said while the car engine idled. "Do we call the cops now or what?"

Ricky shook his head. "Personally, I've seen enough of the police for a while," he replied. "And, man, so have you. We call them *together,* and they're gonna start connecting invisible dots and begin viewing us as 'persons of interest.' And you know what a hassle that can be; particularly if they start spending hours interrogating us about stuff while we need those same precious hours to work out what's going on and save our lives."

"You're right," Grady grudgingly agreed. "We'll just call them if anyone's dead in there."

"Sure, sure," Ricky said. "But for now, let's go investigate."

Grady turned the engine off and they both got out of his car and walked to the front entrance. The welcome sign on the door read, 'WE'RE OPEN.'

"Well, it looks normal even if it is deserted," Ricky said. He pushed the door inward. "It even smells right. I can smell those lovely pizzas baking already."

"I don't like this," Grady said.

With a foot halfway inside the pizza shop, Ricky turned to look at him. "What's bothering you?"

"Listen, I can smell the pizzas cooking in there just like you can. But ask yourself the question I just asked myself: If we're cooking pizzas today, why hasn't anyone called me to come deliver them? And . . . and . . . and . . . you gotta trust me on this one, dude, we *never*— and I mean *never*—like never ever get this many pizza orders this early in the day. And specifically, since this is Monday. Sometimes weekdays, I only deliver one or two pizzas all afternoon, before it picks up after closing hours. But, right now, it smells like Susan is baking enough pies for a Saturday night frat party. But"—and here, Grady tapped his wristwatch for emphasis—"this early in the day?"

Ricky considered that for a while. "You make a good point," he conceded. "Let's investigate anyway." He gestured Grady onward with a wave of his hand. "Come on inside. You can stay out here in front and I'll head on back to the kitchen to see if everyone's in there. If you hear me shout out, you hurry back outside into the parking lot and dial the cops and alert the neighbors."

Ricky gestured outside of the parking lot, at the New State Highway where cars and trucks were busily zipping past and at the deli across the road.

Grady nodded worriedly. "That sounds smart, but I'm scared that the books are smarter than we are. What if everyone's already dead in there?"

Ricky scowled at him. "Dude, just come on inside. At least no one's dead out here; we can both see that much!"

"This is very much against my better judgment," Grady said and followed Ricky inside the pizza shop, into that worryingly rich welcoming aroma of delicious pizza.

"Yeah, this was against my own better judgment also," Ricky quickly admitted once they were both properly inside the pizza shop. "You were right. We should've both waited outside and called the cops to come handle this."

CHAPTER 49

The massive problem that Grady and Ricky had now was that the Bundy's Pizza shop looked different on the inside than it did on the outside.

Grady and Ricky stared around in disbelief.

"How the hell didn't we . . . ?"

What they'd not noticed through the shopfront window while standing out in the parking lot was that there were two severed human heads up on the shop counter.

One of the severed heads belonged to Katie Jensen and the other belonged to Jimmy Hutch. Of the pair of bodies previously connected to the heads there was however, no sign, just lots of blood everywhere. The blood wasn't even dry yet; it still flowed from the dead pair's torn necks and dripped off of the shop counter.

"Well, this explains why they didn't call to let you know if there was work today or not," Ricky said with a sick look on his face. "And if you've not already noticed, that fantastic smell of food that lured us in here has suddenly vanished."

Grady didn't reply. He already had his cellphone out and was dialing 9-1-1.

"No network service," he told Ricky in disgust after three attempts to get through to the emergency services.

Ricky pulled out his own phone and swiped on its screen. "Same thing here."

"I'll dial from outside," Grady said, and gripped the door handle. But then he discovered that he couldn't get the door open.

"Hey, what's the matter?" Ricky asked, stepping over to his side.

"The door's jammed," Grady replied and then, seconds later, both young men leapt back in alarm when the entire shopfront disappeared to be replaced by a wall of what looked like flesh. In addition to its hairy texture, the wall had thick pulsing blood vessels under its skin.

"Did I mention that the room in which Molly's aunt died had a wall made of meat?" Ricky asked in a worried voice.

"Yeah, you did."

"That's fine then."

"The way the shop looked from outside was an illusion," Grady said. "And that smell of pizzas cooking; all of that was simply designed to get us inside the shop."

"You're saying we've been lured into a trap," Ricky said.

"Exactly," Grady agreed. "Our books now have us right where they want us. Let's pray we survive this."

With nothing else to do, and panic threatening to set in, the two young men looked around the shop.

Their apparent underreaction to the presence of the two severed heads on the shop counter was understandable: over the past week both of them had seen their fair share of impossible things, so that now, aside from their concern about their personal wellbeing, it would take something much more creepy that a pair of decapitations to faze them both.

However, the skin wall, with its throbbing veins and smell of human sweat, was almost succeeding in unnerving them. For the most part, Grady and Ricky tried to ignore the skin wall.

"The rest of this front room still looks normal," Ricky observed after a while, gesturing over at the booths and tables in the restaurant area. "So does the passageway to the rear."

Grady pointed along the countertop. "Try calling for help using the landline."

Ricky picked up the landline and listened. "No dial tone," he said and placed it back on the cradle.

Grady sighed. "Oh shit! What are we gonna do now?"

Unconsciously, he staggered back until his back hit the skin wall. And then, galvanized into motion by one of its veins pulsing firmly against his back, he hurried away from it again.

Ricky pointed across the counter, down the passageway to the back. "We'd better try to find another way out of here."

"I doubt it's gonna be that easy," Grady said. "But we've no other option."

He followed Ricky out of the front room.

CHAPTER 50

"Where is everyone?" Ricky asked as they made their cautious way down the corridor. "I mean the living, not the dead."

"Lower your voice," Grady whispered to him. "Look at the floor, if you need to understand why."

Ricky looked at the floor and gulped. All of a sudden they were walking between an aisle of shredded human body parts. Disconnected hands and feet and arms and legs and other body parts that were usually out of sight inside of people abounded on either side of them.

Ricky shuddered and thereafter tried to keep in the middle of the passageway, between the human mess. However, neither he nor Grady could completely avoid stepping in the blood that had streamed from the body parts, and as such they smeared red trails on the floor.

"We've found the rest of Katie and Jimmy," Grady whispered as they stepped cautiously forward. "I wonder what did this to them?"

"Do you really want to know the answer to that?" Ricky asked him. "What else, but those damn books of ours."

"Let's see who's in here," Grady said when they reached the kitchen.

He pushed the kitchen door open, and peeked cautiously inside. The lights were on but the gas ranges and the ovens were all cold and dead.

"Hey, guys, it's Grady," he whispered as loudly as he dared. "Is anyone in here?"

When no one replied, he shut the door again.

But then, before they could move on, Ricky once more pushed the kitchen door open.

"We need to arm ourselves," he explained. "Kitchens are full of weapons."

So they stepped inside the kitchen and began searching. Then, armed with knives and cleavers, they stepped out of the kitchen again and continued on down the passageway.

"Okay, this is the separation between the front and back of the building," Grady told Ricky a few seconds later when they arrived at a transverse corridor. "There are exits on both sides. Choose a direction."

"Left."

They went left and once past Joe's office, stopped because they saw that the skin wall blocked their way out here also. A single fat artery threaded up where the door should have been, pulsing mightily as if full of sufficient blood to flood the entire building.

"I suspect that if we go right we'll meet a similar dead end," Grady pointed out to Ricky, who merely nodded back. "And that most likely goes for the other two exits to this building, the loading dock that opens into the storeroom and the door that leads out back."

After a further defeated glance at the skin wall with its pulsating artery, Ricky leaned against the corridor wall. Then, remembering how Grady had accidentally leaned against the skin wall out front, he stepped away from it again.

"What now?" he asked. "You know the way around here; I don't."

"We need to look for the others—Joe, Susan, and Gina," Grady replied. "Hopefully they'll still be alive." Then he frowned and cocked his head sideways. "Listen," he whispered to Ricky.

Ricky listened. "I can hear something moving," he said after a while. "It's a weird scratching noise like . . . I don't know what it sounds like; it just sounds really creepy." He listened some more. "Sounds like it's coming from the back area."

"Back there's the bosses' living quarters," Grady explained in a hushed voice. "Let's go. That's likely one of the other three."

"Or the thing that killed those two out front," Ricky told him.

But still, after a final nervous look at the living wall that blocked their way out, Ricky followed Grady out of the side corridor towards the living quarters at the back of the building.

CHAPTER 51

The two young men had barely gotten the door to the apartment section of the building open when Susan Bundy came charging pell-mell out of it.

"Run!" she yelled, as she knocked them both out of the way.

Grady and Ricky took one look at the panic on her face and then turned and dashed after her.

As they followed Susan back towards the front of the building, they got a good look at her and saw that she was totally covered in blood and was also holding a gun. Those two facts, plus the fact that the morbidly obese woman was outstripping them both in the speed stakes, hammered the urgency of the situation into both of their perplexed consciousnesses.

While running they could hear something in pursuit of them. But it was only after they'd reached the front restaurant area of the pizza shop, and had turned around to latch the access door to the rear passage, that they saw what exactly they were fleeing from.

"What the fuck?" Ricky practically yelled in fright after their single brief glimpse of their pursuer, before they'd slammed the door shut on it and were latching it shut.

After they got the door safely locked, the thing on its other side slammed into it. The impact rocked the door on its hinges, but it held. The thing hit the door again, and they heard wood splintering.

Hearing this, Grady and Ricky looked at one another in alarm. Then their four eyes riveted on the door latch, which shuddered on each jarring impact like it might pop its screws out of the jamb. Grady had good reason to worry about this, because the latch was a flimsy one that wasn't really designed for security, because, seeing as the passageway door lacked a window in its upper half, it was mostly left open anyway.

But to their relief, the creature on the other side of the door seemed to have reached the limits of its ability to exert force on the opening. It didn't attack the door again, but they still heard it pacing about outside there, making horrible slobbering and scratching sounds.

"I believe we're safe for the moment," Grady told Ricky. Then they both turned around to stare at Susan.

"What the hell was that thing!?" Ricky yelled at her.

In the meantime, Susan was staring at the two heads on the counter, and shivering and gibbering and gnawing the knuckles of her left hand, while waving the gun in her right hand wildly around like she desperately needed a target to shoot at.

Then she turned and ran at the skin wall that now blocked off the parking lot and highway from view, and while screaming, began beating on it with both hand and gun.

The blood on her body clearly wasn't hers, and oddly seemed to be wet in some places and dry in others. The watching young men soon realized that the damp patches were caused by Susan's sweating.

"Susan, what is that thing out there?" Ricky asked her again, gently this time.

Susan now turned to reply him. She had a look of madness in her eyes.

"It's Joe and Gina!" she whispered harshly.

"What?" Grady and Ricky asked together.

"How the hell can that *thing* be Joe and Gina?" Grady added.

"Yes, it's them!" Susan insisted. When they continued gaping at her in disbelief, she pulled a copy of 'How to Succeed in Life' from somewhere amidst her bloody clothing and waved it at them.

"After I sent you and Katie home yesterday afternoon, I found them both dead," she explained. "I dunno who killed them or what, but . . . Well, at first I was gonna call the cops, but then I decided to try out the ritual in this book, but when I did it, instead of being showered with money and fame, the pieces of their bodies joined together again and . . . the damn thing has been chasing me about since yesterday."

She sagged after saying this and both young men saw that she was completely exhausted, on the borderline of having both a physical and a nervous collapse.

Grady and Ricky glanced at each other, and then Grady asked: "Susan, where did you get that book you're holding?"

"Someone forgot it here," she said. She looked like she was going to say more, but then her terror apparently overcame her again.

"Listen," she told them in an out-of-breath voice, "we need to figure out a way out of here. This damn meat wall runs around the whole building now."

"Didn't look like it from the outside," Ricky said.

Susan rolled her eyes at him and wobbled unsteadily on her feet. "Yeah, yeah, that's what they want us all to think. So, from outside the place looks normal." She gestured at the severed heads on the counter. "But once you step inside here like Katie and Jimmy did—"

"Hold on and backtrack a bit," Grady said. "You just mentioned a 'they' wanting us to think this place was still the same. Who are 'they?'"

"Yeah, great question," Ricky agreed.

Susan looked from one to the other of them and then shook her head. "Guys, I honestly don't know. But I'm figuring someone sent us the books. I'm saying 'us' because I later saw that Gina had one too." She began looking agitated again, and now sweat was practically oozing out of the pores of her large face. "Listen, you guys: we can figure out who's responsible for this mess later, but as for right now"—and here she gestured weakly toward the locked access door to the rear passage—"at the moment, escaping that damn monster that's trying to get in here is my priority. Neither of you know what that thing will do if it catches us." Now she gestured instead at the severed heads on the shop counter. "I've seen it in action—what do you think shredded their bodies like that and spread them over the passageway?" She waved her gun wildly. "And I've also shot it lotsa times, but it won't die."

Now Susan frowned and cocked her head sideways. "Can you hear it out there? Can you still hear it?"

Both men listened like she was doing. "Can't hear a thing," Ricky said finally, with Grady nodding his agreement. "I think it's left."

Susan smirked and wagged a plump index finger at them. "Oh, no no no, boys. That what it *wants* us to think. It's still out there, tryin' to find a way inside here, so that it can—"

Then Susan looked up and screamed.

CHAPTER 52

Grady looked up when Susan did and almost screamed too.

The thing they'd fled from was now up on the ceiling.

It dangled there above them like a giant spider that a mad scientist had inflated until it exploded, and which he'd then repaired using human body parts. It was a mass of arms and legs and raw meat and shredded flesh and skin.

Grady identified individual parts of Joe Bundy and Gina Luz as components of the creature. The hairy arms and legs and hands and feet were unmistakably Joe's, while the hairless set of limbs and extremities just as obviously came from Gina. The monster had no head, but it had a lot of mouths spread across its impossible body that were filled with teeth that were really cracked bones, like it ate with its ribcages.

Grady had no idea how the monster had gotten into the restaurant from the hallway, because aside from the front entrance, the locked passageway door was the only access to the rear of the building.

Did it crawl through the wall or fall through the ceiling or simply materialize in here?

But this was hardly the time to reason that out.

The flesh monster had appeared spread out above both Susan and Ricky, but it was closer to Susan and so she would have been its natural choice of victim.

But Susan had clearly been expecting something of this sort to happen. Immediately she saw the monster overhead, she reacted fast.

Quick as a flash, she turned her gun on Ricky and shot him in the belly.

What the fuck? Grady wondered in shock.

"You crazy bitch," Ricky howled at Susan in pain and anger, then he looked at Grady in surprise. "Dude, your boss just shot me."

"Why'd you do that?" Grady asked Susan.

"Get real," Susan told him. "The monster is hungry and it doesn't care who it eats. Better your friend than you and me."

Above them, the monster stuck to the ceiling was acting very agitated now. Thought it had no eyes that any of them could see, it was clearly readying itself to attack, guided by whatever infernal instincts motivated it. In the meantime, it added to the meaty smell in the restaurant and dripped disgusting fluids on the floor.

"Hey, stop! Don't do that!" Grady told Susan when he saw that her finger was curling on the trigger of her gun again.

But, with a cold smile on her lips, Susan shot Ricky in the belly again. This time Ricky went down to one knee. Then he forced himself back upright and staggered towards Susan to attack her with the knives he was holding.

Seeing Ricky approaching her, Susan attempted to shoot him a third time, but this time her gun clicked empty.

But just as Ricky reached Susan to stab her, the monster came down for him. It fell from the ceiling in a flurry of arms and legs and gnashing teeth.

Susan Bundy leapt away to safety, and all of a sudden, most of Ricky Lawson was buried underneath the impossible hellish thing, and Ricky was screaming blue murder.

With the monster a living blanket covering him, Ricky collapsed to the floor, where he kicked and flailed beneath the raw meat creature, with just his hands visible outside of it.

Susan now looked pointedly at Grady.

"See?" she told him in a satisfied voice. "We're both safe for a while now. By feeding it your friend, I just bought us both some time. Now, let's get out of here before—"

But then, either as the result of a blind instinct on Ricky's part that sensed something nearby that he could grasp on to pull himself free from his current torment, or as the conscious result of anger directed in the direction of her voice, Ricky stretched out a hand and grabbed Susan's ankle.

Scarily, it may even have been that the meat monster had managed to connect itself to Ricky's nerves, and was now using his hands to achieve its own deadly purposes, as if he'd now become an extension of its own hideous body.

Before Susan could bend to free herself from Ricky's grip, he jerked on her leg so violently that she was upended and landed on her back on the floor.

The impact only stunned Susan for a few seconds, but that was long enough for the meat monster to grab a hold of her also with two of its hands and hold her fast.

It appeared to thin and divide now, with half of its mass flowing over Susan instead of Ricky.

Susan, who'd somehow maintained her grip on her gun when she'd hit the floor, instantly dropped the empty weapon and began fighting to break free from the monster's clutches.

Ricky had stopped screaming now and Grady could easily see why. Those parts of the hell creature that had flowed off of Ricky's body revealed that just the skeleton remained beneath it. Those of its mouths that had covered him were chewing meat and dripping blood on the floor.

Those of its mouths that had reached Susan spread open wide and bit deeply into her.

Her cool murderous reserve now completely vanished, Susan began screaming at Grady: "Help me, man! Help me! It's eating me!"

"Oh shit!" Grady gasped.

Then, raising the knives that he'd been holding since leaving the kitchen, he hurried towards Susan to see if he could get her away from the demonic creature.

But immediately he neared the monster, it split itself again, and extended several of its mouths towards him.

It was insane: one of what Grady assumed was Gina's breasts (probably her left one as there was an armpit on its left side) suddenly split open to reveal, not soft jelly-like fat, but long and sharp teeth that instantly snapped at him.

Grady was forced to leap back to safety beside the shut door to the rear, from where he watched the mass of meat and limbs eat Susan Bundy while she screamed and screamed and screamed.

Finally, unable to bear the noise of Susan's agony any longer, Grady unlatched the door to the rear and ran out of there.

CHAPTER 53

Unnerved now, Grady hurried through the Bundy's house, looking for an exit, any exit. Just somewhere that the skin covering hadn't reached yet. Anywhere would do.

Finally, however, he realized that what Susan had told he and Ricky was true—the skin wall extended all the way around the house.

He sat down where he was then, on the toilet seat in Joe's bathroom, and fought to get a grip on himself. Still, he had tears in his eyes.

Dammit! Why the hell would Susan shoot Ricky like that? That's just . . .

Then he realized that his cellphone was ringing.

He got it out of his pocket and saw that it was Molly calling.

He quickly accepted the call: "Molly, thank God you can reach me. We're—"

"Oh, I'm so, so so so so glad I finally got a hold of you," Molly gushed into his ear. "I've been calling you for an hour now. Grady, we're in deep shit!"

Grady sighed and replied, "You don't know a quarter of it."

"Hey, is Ricky with you there? I've been calling him, but I can't get through either, but he'd left me your number in case of that, so . . . Is he there with you?"

"Ricky's dead," Grady told Molly in a slow and broken voice. "Something terrible got him."

"Oh, shit," Molly said and fell silent for a while.

Grady listened to the silent phone for close to a minute before speaking.

"Hey, Molly, are you still there? Listen, there's something about this place now—I don't have the time to go into details, but I'm at the pizza shop and its transformed and—"

"I'm really upset right now but I'll be okay," Molly interrupted him in a sad and miserable voice. "Grady, I'm not surprised that Ricky's dead. From what I can tell from what I've discovered, we're all marked for death too. Right now the walls of Ricky's place are looking funny. In fact they look like . . ."

CHAPTER 54

The outer wall of Ricky's house now seemed to be covered with human skin. And not just any sort of human skin either, but human skin with a similar texture to that of the book 'How to Succeed in Life.'

At the moment, Ricky's place had no external openings anymore, just that creepy covering of skin.

Molly had searched through the entire house, seeking a way outside, but she'd found none. Each exit had ceased to exist; all that faced her each time she'd arrived at where either a door or a window should have been was hairy twitching pale flesh that had dark blood vessels beating under its surface.

Right now, Molly Woods was terrified. Yes, she was horribly shocked and saddened by Ricky's death, but for the time being she was managing to compartmentalize her grief. Molly was doing this because she realized she had no choice in the matter. From what she'd discovered, she and Grady and Kayla and all of the others who had copies of the book 'How to Succeed in Life' were living on borrowed time.

All that grieving for Ricky would accomplish now for Molly would be to shorten her own share of that fast-vanishing time.

What Molly had uncovered during her research was horrible.

"Listen," she told Grady over the phone, "This is all some kinda game. No no no, I mean it's a *competition,* like a game show kind of thing."

"What the hell?" Grady asked. "How do you . . . Just go on talking. I'll hold off with the questions."

"Yeah," Molly agreed. "Keep your questions to a minimum. I've a lot to tell you, and I dunno how much time we've got left."

"I'm listening."

Before going on, Molly arranged her laptop so that she had all of the facts she needed at her fingertips. The internet had stopped working when the wall turned to skin and hadn't come back on when her phone resumed working, but those webpages that she'd already opened up still retained their content.

"Okay, this is sort of a *demonic* competition," she explained. "How it works is that one person finds a copy of the book 'How to Succeed in Life' and then other people connected to that person start to receive copies too. Those copies can come in the mail, by courier, can be found lying on the sidewalk, be forgotten by a customer at the nail salon or whatever. You get this part of it?"

Grady laughed. "Oh, I do."

His laughter unsettled Molly, who felt that at the moment, it was very inappropriate. "Stop laughing. This is serious."

"You've no idea how serious it is."

"No, Grady, *you're* the one who has no idea how serious things are." Frowning, Molly went on: "Now, of course, after everyone's gotten a copy of the book, they're all expected to read it. As to who sets the rules or moderates things or . . . Oh, shit, I forgot something." Molly tapped the touch-sensitive screen of her laptop and brought a particular page with occult symbols to the fore. "Yeah, this book we've got is part of something much larger called the Necromantica."

"The Necromantica? You mean *necromancy*, like in communicating with dead people?"

"Yeah, something like that. Although, it's more than just talking to the dead. Actually, a better description of the Necromantica is to call it the LOTUS; pronounced the same way as the flower."

"What's that mean?"

"LOTUS means 'Library of the Unholy Sciences.' According to my research, the LOTUS is an endless compendium or collection of all of the most evil books in existence."

"Hey, hey! The book I found is too small to be an entire library."

"That's because you only found one volume of it." Molly peered closely at the laptop screen. "Actually, 'How to Succeed in Life' is LOTUS Volume 82514."

She heard Grady gasp. "What? There's that many of them?"

"Just listen," she went on urgently. "My whole point in telling you this is so you'll understand what we're dealing with here. This isn't just some internet goth girls' witchery gone wrong—it's part of an eternal evil—something that's been around since antiquity, way way way before Christ."

"I get that now," Grady replied. "Go on, hurry up. Just cut to the chase. I don't know how long I've got before it . . . it . . ."

"Okay, okay," Molly agreed. "I'll attempt to rush this. I just don't want to leave out anything important."

While speaking she kept glancing around her living room. She had the sense that she wasn't alone in the house anymore. And also, she'd already made the very unnerving connection that this house's flesh wall was exactly like the flesh wall in the room where her Aunt Melda had died.

"Now listen," Molly said. "Like I was saying earlier, it works like this: one person finds the book, and then the book somehow multiplies itself to the most important people in that person's life. So, take this case for instance: you found the book and then your family gets copies and also your best friend and maybe your employer also and . . . I'm certain you get the point I'm making."

"Oh, so that's why Susan and Gina got copies too," Grady replied.

That surprised Molly. "They did? No, no, let's not get sidetracked. There's more: So, once you get your own copy of the book, you're like, automatically enrolled into the game show or competition, whether you like it or not, and whether you know it or not."

"What if you refuse to play?"

Molly tapped another page to the front on her laptop. "You *can't* refuse. Well you can, but . . . Okay, here's how it goes: you can't be forced to play against your will, but it's fatal if you refuse to. Some people quit, they refuse to play the game once they discover what the stakes are, or if something they deem too precious to part with is demanded from them. Apparently, the game doesn't like this attitude, and it kills such people quickly and messily, to make an example to the other players."

"That's likely what happened to pops," Grady said sadly. "My dad wasn't the kinda guy to get involved in any demon-worship shenanigans."

"Yeah, I think so too," Molly agreed. "Your dad refused to play and so the book got him out of the way."

"Did you find out anything about who's responsible for this? Like who runs it, or who set it up?"

Molly shook her head, though there was no one there to watch her do so. "Nada. Apparently, it's being going on since antiquity. Also, the problem is that some of the books in the LOTUS are so evil and also so powerful that they can easily go into business for themselves. It's apparently like literary AI—the books become self-aware and then become bored with having nothing to do. So they create situations like this one to boost their egos and make themselves relevant in human affairs." Molly smirked. "Oddly, there's a suggestion that in this case LOTUS Vol: 82514 may have become virulently active on the internet simply because, in this day and age, it's jealous of the number of self-help books in print. In that sense it views itself as a neglected idol."

"Where the fuck does that leave us then? What does it expect us to do? Worship it?"

Molly had to laugh at that. "In a sense, yes. We worship it by competing like it demands."

"Molly, why do you—and me also now—keep saying 'It' like there's just one copy?"

"Because apparently there is only one master copy. It makes as many copies of itself as it needs to, but they're all just the same single book."

"That's crazy."

"Grady, at the moment I'm trapped inside of a house that has a skin wall with hair and throbbing arteries or veins or whatever and that smells like an unwashed drunk. How's that for crazy?"

"Sorry, I kinda overlooked that. Go on. Please, hurry up."

"Now, onto the book's contents. Basically, they're just a series of demonic rituals that grant extreme wealth and fame to those who complete them. The thing is, there are different rituals in the book; what you see and read apparently depends on the sort of person you are; your character and personality."

"Okay, so we aren't all expected to perform the same ritual?"

"No. But we're all in similar danger, as far as I can tell. This evil competition is a race against time. Once one person completes the ritual, the other players, or rather participants in the game are then regarded as sacrifices, and the book then mops them all up to enhance the winner's value. Actually, the losers are considered payments for the winner's success."

"That's *very* bad."

"Yes, it is," Molly agreed. "Really bad for us. Here's the thing, Grady. You need to work out who's activated the ritual. I think someone has either begun or completed it and once that's been done, the only way out is to kill that person, which resets the game to . . . Hey, man, hold on a minute, I'm hearing something weird."

"Hey, be careful," Grady told her over the phone. "You've no idea how insane this can get."

Molly had to laugh at that. Her laughter was a cold and irritating noise that even to herself sounded morbid and hopeless. "Grady, I already told you, I'm surrounded by a hairy skin wall. And yesterday, I saw an old guy's decapitated head crying out in pain, right before his wife double-slit her own throat right in front of me. Stop telling me about crazy."

"Just be careful. I'm serious."

Trembling now, Molly picked up her phone, got to her feet, and walked towards the kitchen. That was where she'd heard the sound coming from.

She reached the kitchen and peered in. "Hey, who's in here?"

But the kitchen was empty. The disgusting skin wall that had sealed off the external world was still in place.

"No one's in here," she told Grady, as she peered both high and low in the kitchen and even looked behind the kitchen door. "But I'm certain I heard some noises."

"Maybe you did. Maybe Ricky has rats in the house," Grady suggested.

"I guess," Molly agreed and turned around.

Then she froze in shock and her fingers seemed to go numb around the cellphone.

"You?" she gasped at the shadowy figure that was now standing in front of her. "What are you doing here? How'd you get in here?"

"Hey, who's there with you?" Grady asked her in an alarmed voice. "Who is it?"

But the person who'd somehow just appeared in Ricky's house was holding an axe, and the axe was already descending towards Molly's head.

"It's . . ." was all Molly could reply Grady before the axe spit her head completely in two.

CHAPTER 55

Grady heard the sickening wet 'Thunk!' of something striking hard close to the phone and Molly's accompanying yelp of pain. And then there was silence, an absence of noise that was followed by the sound of two things striking the floor, one of them dull and heavy, the other noise higher-pitched.

That was both Molly and her cellphone biting the dust, Grady realized and a sinking sensation filled him. *She's dead too now. Shit.*

He looked at his cellphone. Unsurprisingly, considering what he knew now, all network service had again vanished on Molly's passing.

We're trapped inside of the book's personal universe, Grady understood. *Molly was able to contact me here only because the book permitted her to. It wanted me to know what she'd found out. But why is that? So I can properly participate in this crazy competition? Or is it so that I can end the game in my own favor?*

He put his cellphone away in his pocket. All through his phone conversation with Molly, he'd remained sitting on the toilet seat in Joe's bathroom, but now he got up and peered outside into the attached bedroom.

Having not really paid attention to it while fleeing through the house searching for an escape route, Grady was shocked now by the room's condition.

Joe's bedroom was a mess of blood and pieces of body skin and tissue, with tatters of bloody fabric—shreds of jeans, parts of a bra, the tee shirt that Gina had earlier been wearing but now exploded into pieces—spread everywhere. A bloody meat cleaver lay in the middle of the bedroom rug, which itself was soggy with partially dried blood.

As with the rest of the house, one wall (in this case the wall that also sealed off the bathroom Grady had sat down in) was a throbbing surface of seemingly human flesh.

This bloody bedroom was clearly where Joe and Gina had both died—and where Susan had created her hellish monster.

Grady frowned at the mess everywhere. *I don't believe Susan found Joe and Gina dead anymore. I think she came home, caught them having sex, and killed them both. And afterwards she realized that she could use their corpses to perform the book's ritual.*

He grimaced. *That thing like a basketball over there in the corner looks like it might be Joe's head—but I'm not about to go over there and make certain of it.*

Thereafter, seeing and sensing no danger to himself in Joe's bedroom, and hearing nothing alarming out beyond it, Grady walked through the bedroom, out into the living room, and sat down there.

His absentminded realization that Gina Luz's own severed head lay over against the DVD rack made little impression on him. (After all, his subconscious reasoned, if, like Joe's head, Gina's head also wasn't part of the crazy thing that had killed Ricky and Susan, then it had to be somewhere else.)

Also, he paid no further attention to the exterior living room wall, that extensive hairy and windowless expanse of human skin that demanded to be noticed because of the sheer impossibility of its existence.

Grady suddenly felt like something was missing from this scenario. What could that possibly be? And now that he thought about it, that 'something' had been missing from his life for a while now.

Oh yes, I should have a copy of the book responsible for all of this on me.

But when he patted down his pockets to see if this was so, he discovered that they were all empty. Apparently, now that the book 'How to Succeed in Life' had lured and herded him inside here, it had abandoned him to his own devices.

Or maybe it's been keeping watch outside of the pizza joint to ensure that none of us escape. And so far, none of us have.

Grady considered the number of dead people—the startling number of people who'd died since yesterday morning.

I guess this means the game is now winding down to a close.

What Molly had told him over the phone now hummed in his mind like an overloaded electric transformer.

Molly said that someone either activated or completed the ritual, and that their doing so made everyone else sacrifices. That 'someone' has to be one of those who either has or had a copy of the book.

And so, sitting on Joe's living room couch, Grady Burke now began a process of elimination:

For a start, how many people got copies of the book? Let's assume Pops had a copy. I got one, Kayla got one. That's our entire family. Then, on to friends: Ricky got one too. I'm assuming Gina got one simply cuz I like her. But why did Susan get a copy of 'How to Succeed in Life' too? Maybe because, of my two employers, she likes me more than Joe does? Or was the book perhaps actually intended for him?

Grady shrugged. *Okay now, time to match the dead to the books. Who's left alive?*

Pops is dead and so are Ricky and Molly, Gina, Susan and Joe. No, neither Molly or Joe had copies, they were just collateral damage, as I think were also Ricky's landlady and her husband, Kayla's two porno friends, and both Katie and Jimmy, my two hapless colleagues-in-pizza. I mean, from what we hear of the guy, the devil's never been one to turn down a few extra souls.

Grady frowned at his own bad joke.

So, lemme start again, this time leaving out those who didn't have copies: Pops is dead and so are Ricky, Gina and Susan, who all received copies of 'How to Succeed in Life' or LOTUS 82514 as Molly said it's also called.

This leaves just me and Kayla as the only two survivors.

And that means Susan was the one who activated the spell, and so . . . But . . . but no, Susan said something went wrong with the ritual she performed. We saw that clearly. Instead of the promised results, Susan created the monster that then killed her.

Here, Grady scratched his chin and frowned. He wondered what Susan's monster was up to at the moment, and if it was already searching for him too.

This possibility really scared Grady, but then he remembered how Susan had said that feeding Ricky to the hellish creature had bought them both some time.

Exactly how Susan could have known that such was the case puzzled Grady. It seemed to him that Susan couldn't have known that her murderous action would produce that result, except if, rather than the monster attacking Katie and Jimmy on its own, Susan had intentionally fed both of them to the evil meat creature (most likely to facilitate her own escape from it), and then noted the results of her doing so.

Which, after seeing her cold-bloodedly shoot Ricky like she did, isn't a farfetched conjecture. And that means that Susan's own death must've in turn purchased additional time for me.

Grady frowned.

Hopefully, her death has bought me enough extra time to unriddle this mess I'm trying to figure out. Now where was I?

Okay, yeah . . . Susan's own spectacular failure at the ritual clearly means that someone else activated the ritual before she did, thus rendering her own attempt invalid. But who did so?

The only two survivors are Kayla and myself. And if I didn't do it, and I KNOW that I didn't, then the only possible person who could have either begun or finished off the ritual was . . . Kayla?

Grady's eyes widened in surprise.

Did Kayla perform the ritual? Is that why she wasn't harmed but others at her farewell orgy were? What else am I missing?

Then, he remembered something else and his eyes widened even more:

"Oh, yes, it is Kayla," he thought aloud. "Molly definitely recognized the person who killed her. She was gonna tell me who it was when she was killed."

And then, suddenly, his older sister was standing right there in Joe Bundy's living room with him.

CHAPTER 56

Grady was shaken by Kayla's current physical appearance.

Kayla looked deranged, like a demon. She was even more blood-soaked than Susan had been. Her blonde hair was so bloody that she could easily be mistaken for a redhead with pale highlights.

As proof of Grady's recent realization, Kayla was carrying a bloodstained axe.

Most disconcerting of all, Grady's older and trans sister had an erection. Kayla was dressed only in a long pink tee shirt that descended over her hips, and her penis stuck out stiffly in front of her, raising the front of the tee shirt several inches.

As a final obscene/surreal touch, Kayla's tee shirt read: 'Pu**y Is Overrated; Try A** Instead.'

Grady really didn't know what to think. He still had one knife with him and Kayla wasn't making any attempt at attacking him and so he relaxed slightly, ready to move in his own defense if she did attack him.

As to how Kayla had suddenly materialized here in front of him, Grady didn't bother considering.

What's the point in demanding a rational explanation to impossible things, when you're surrounded by living walls of flesh?

Kayla walked forward till she was standing right in front of Grady.

"Did you enjoy killing Molly so much that you got a boner?" Grady asked her.

Kayla laughed. "You know I never liked that girl."

"At least now we know for certain that she didn't witch pops to death. Why'd you do it, sis? Pops loved us both to death."

Kayla frowned at him. "Grady, I didn't kill our daddy."

"I don't believe you."

Kayla set down her axe on the coffee table and then sat beside Grady on the living room couch.

"No, li'l brother, I didn't kill pops," she said. "Pops died because he refused to do what the book wanted him to. That pissed the book off and so it killed him. Once I realized this, I decided to do what the book wanted."

Grady nodded. "That makes sense. So then, you're saying that those porno orgy deaths weren't the accidents that they seemed to be?"

Kayla nodded. "That was what the book wanted. All I had to do was set things up and have sex as normal, and the book would do the rest. It would itself claim the two people whose souls it wanted." Kayla ran bloody fingernails across her perfect lips, and then twirled bloodied blonde hair between her fingers. "I had no idea it was all gonna be so bloody though."

"Okay," Grady agreed. "And after that?"

"Molly already told you the rest. She was right. Once I did what the book wanted, everyone else who'd got a copy of 'How to Succeed in Life' had become a sacrifice."

"So what happens now?" Grady asked as his gaze flitted aside to latch on Gina's head. "You and I, sis, we're the only two left. Everyone else is dead."

And that was when Grady felt a terrible pain in his right side. He looked down and saw that Kayla had stabbed him. She'd driven the knife in so deep that only the handle stuck out of Grady's body.

Then, as the realization struck Grady that she'd dropped the axe on the coffee table merely to lull him into a false sense of security, Kayla dragged the knife sideways through Grady's belly, with its razor-honed blade slicing apart every internal organ in its path. Grady tried to get up and get away from her, but she leaned forward onto him, keeping him firmly in place on the couch, the pale upholstery of which was now wetting and reddening with his blood. She also kept the knife deep inside his body, twisting it sideways to cut something else loose inside of him.

"Why?" Grady gasped as agony filled his body like fire. "I'm your *brother*. We're both rich now with the money that pops left us."

"Not rich enough by half," she whispered in his ear, her voice gentle and caressing. "I need to kill you to finish this and become *really* successful and that's what I'm doing now."

By now, feeling all of the blood leaving his body, and with his torso wracked with pain, Grady knew that he was dying.

But dying at his own sister's hands seemed insane. He and Kayla had always had such a great and loving sibling relationship; and now this?

"Has turning trans turned you totally psycho too?" he questioned her as he felt himself going cold.

Kayla actually seemed angered by the question. "This ain't about gender or sexuality; this is entirely about money," she replied testily, with her lips brushing his ear. "Being trans doesn't mean I can't be greedy too. Whoever said straight or cis people should have all of the fun!?"

Grady forced a mixture of words and blood through his lips. He was fading fast now, and knew that his only chance of survival lay with somehow appealing to Kayla's sense of reason, that was if she still had any left.

"But we're sister and brother, we can share!" he protested.

And now, Kayla pulled slightly back and shook her head at him. She had a hint of sadness in her eyes. "Sorry, bro, but like Molly already told you, the ritual doesn't permit sharing. It's sinner takes all."

And then, Kayla Burke pulled the knife out of Grady's body.

But Grady died before she could stab him again.

CHAPTER 57

Once Grady was dead, Kayla got down to the final part of the magic ritual.

This part involved first cutting Grady's heart out of his body.

Kayla worked fast. According to the book, she needed to get the organ out of him while it was still warm.

Not being the kitchen expert Susan Grundy had been, it took Kayla a while to extract her brother's heart from his chest.

However, because of the magic coming from the flesh walls, Grady's heart was still hot and steaming when Kayla got it out of him. And even though the purple organ's owner was long dead now, the heart itself was still beating.

Her own heart beating fast in keen anticipation of her successful life hereafter, Kayla held Grady's heart up in front of her for a few seconds.

Then she picked up her knife again and punched a deep hole in the organ, one that extended from top to bottom.

And finally, just like the ritual demanded, Kayla stuck her erect penis (its relentlessly turgid state the result of four tablets of Viagra and nothing to do with hatred of Molly Woods) into Grady's heart, and then she used his heart as a masturbation sleeve.

This definitely isn't something I'd recommend to anyone else, she thought while doing this.

Keeping a firm grip on the still-throbbing heart while rhythmically penetrating it was difficult because both her hands and the organ itself were slippery with blood.

If this had been any normal type of situation, Kayla would have been very concerned about the amount of DNA evidence she was leaving at this crime scene.

But now she smiled and gasped in sexual pleasure.

In this case, there's no problem at all. The book has assured me that it's cleaning up after me. Let the cops search for a million years, they'll never find a single shred of evidence that I was ever here today or at Ricky's house either, or that I was in any way involved in this massacre.

Kayla kept thrusting into her brother's heart until she ejaculated into it. And then, taking care not to spill any of her semen out of the heart, she picked up her copy of 'How to Succeed in Life' off of the coffee table, opened it up, and read out the spell on the last page.

Kayla had read the book so many times now that its arcane language seemed like English to her.

She finished the spell and laughed when Grady's semen-filled heart vanished from her hand.

"Oh, yes," Kayla thought with delight as she too began fading from the Bundy's living room. "It's done. My new life begins now."

She cast a single regretful look at her brother's butchered corpse and vanished.

EPILOGUE

Jerry Wedley arrived at the house at a quarter to midnight. This was his last pizza run for the day, and after this he was on his way home.

Once he'd confirmed that this was the correct address, Jerry got off of his motorbike and, hot bag in hand, walked up the house driveway.

Jerry reached the front door and pressed the doorbell.

And here the oddness began.

Right after Jerry pressed the doorbell, the front door swung wide open. Jerry found himself staring into the house.

Jerry was startled.

Hey, hey, I know I just heard someone unlock the door. But . . . but there's no one here!

But then, Jerry decided that wasn't anything to worry about.

"Hello, I've a pizza for Ms. Lane!" Jerry called out.

For some odd reason that he couldn't explain, Jerry knew he'd get no reply to this statement.

"Hello. Pizza delivery for Ms. Lane!" Jerry called out again, louder this time. All of a sudden, he was getting a weird tingling sensation down his spine, a creepy feeling which didn't sit well with him at all. Now he just wanted someone to come to the door and collect their pizza and pay him. They didn't even have to tip him. Jerry simply wanted to be well away from here in the shortest time possible.

He was about calling out again, when a woman's voice replied: "Please come on in, I'm busy in the kitchen."

Figuring that that had to be Ms. Lane talking to him, Jerry walked on into the house.

"Just come on through the living room," Ms. Lane directed.

In the living room the television was on. His urgency to leave slightly dulled now that Ms. Lane had replied him, Jerry paused a moment to watch TV.

Onscreen, a gorgeous blonde woman was being interviewed.

"And so, Kayla, please tell our studio audience and viewers at home your tips for success."

While Kayla replied, a banner unfurled at the bottom of the screen with the info: "Kayla Burke, just voted most influential internet personality."

Jerry had heard of Kayla Burke. As far as he could tell, she was simply another young woman with too much money at her disposal. She was apparently worth a half billion dollars or something ridiculous like that. A friend had told him she was transgender too. And that she used to be a porno actress.

Jerry wondered how she'd gotten so rich in such a short time. Because honestly, he couldn't help but feel a trifle envious of her. Yes, Jerry felt envious of Kayla Burke.

It won't hurt me none tho' if she has some good success tips that can help me boost my own income.

"Well, it all began with a book I found somewhere," Kayla said in a sweet voice. "I don't even remember where I found the book."

"What was the title of the book?" the middle-aged male interviewer asked.

"It was titled 'How to Succeed in Life,' " Kayla Burke replied. Then she laughed: "Yeah, I know the title sounds cheesy, like a million other self-help manuals, but it really worked. It REALLY did; for me at least. I mean, it helped me turn my entire life around. And, believe me, I badly needed that turnaround. You can imagine what sort of a mess I was in after both my father and my brother died so tragically and in such a short period—within days of each other, and both under such macabre circumstances. I felt cursed, like I'd be the next one to die, but then I found that book and since then—"

"You can bring the pizza into the kitchen," Ms. Lane called out.

"Okay, I'm coming," Jerry replied.

So Jerry Wedley left off watching the interview and resumed his walk to the kitchen. But maybe his attention was still distracted by Kayla Burke's voice, because all of a sudden, Jerry's foot snagged on something on the carpet and he almost both dropped the hot bag containing the pizza he was delivering and went flying to boot.

But he righted himself just in time.

Once he was certain of his balance, Jerry looked down to see what had tripped him up.

He was surprised. The only thing on the floor that could have tripped him up was something that couldn't possibly have done so.

Jerry reached down and picked up the small pamphlet. It had a leathery feel to it that was very unpleasant and that once more made him feel like he wanted to leave this house as fast as possible.

Don't be a pussy, man. It's just a book. But how the hell can this flat little thing have tripped me up?

Jerry didn't bother answering the question. He simply dropped the book on top of the hot bag and proceeded into the kitchen.

Once through the kitchen entrance, Jerry froze in place and just managed not to flee in terror.

Yes, Ms. Lane was in her kitchen. But . . .

Ms. Lane's body was draped over the kitchen island and her head was missing. But that wasn't all. A short but thick trail of blood led from the dead woman's neck across the kitchen floor to the kitchen counter . . . and to the microwave.

Fearing for his sanity now (and somehow miraculously managing not to drop the pizza bag) Jerry slowly stepped towards the microwave, taking care not to bloody his sneakers in the process. This was sort of like a gruesome motor accident that you just had to see; you really should keep driving on past it, but nonetheless you couldn't look away from it.

So Jerry walked up to the microwave and looked inside it.

The microwave was on and something was inside it cooking.

While Jerry was still coming to terms with the fact that Mrs. Lane's severed head was cooking in her own microwave oven, the head parted its lips and spoke to him:

"Thanks for bringing in the pizza, "Mrs. Lane said, amidst the pops and crackles of her roasting flesh. "Just give me a minute and I'll be done in here and come attend to you."

Jerry turned around on the spot and ran out of the house and called the cops.

Of course, the cops never believed that Jerry had actually heard and even seen the dead woman talking to him. Just like they didn't believe his story that the front door had seemingly opened up to admit him of its own accord.

According to the police, Ms. Lane's front door must have left open by the psychos who'd murdered her and afterwards microwaved her head, and who had also cut out her heart and taken it away with them.

"Yeah, yeah, I guess you guys are right," Jerry simply nodded to all this, and finally arrived home at 2 a.m. in the morning.

And that was when he realized that somehow he'd also brought the little book he'd found in the murdered woman's living room—the book he'd somehow almost tripped over—back home with him.

Looking at it now, Jerry Wedley couldn't make either head or tail of it. The book was entirely made of a sort of creepy skin-like leather, and the writing on it was all in some writing he'd never seen before in his life.

Even Egyptian hieroglyphics make more sense than this, he thought.

He flipped through the book and it was all more of the same nonsense.

Maybe it's a clue to the murders, he thought finally. *I'll hand it in to the cops in the morning.*

But then, come morning, something about the book prevented Jerry from handing it over to law enforcement.

Instead, he took it down to breakfast with him and showed it to his wife Heather and his teenage daughter Traci.

And it was his daughter Traci who all of a sudden told him: "Dad, I don't know how I know this, but this book is titled 'How to Succeed in Life.' I mean it, dad: that's what this writing on the cover says."

Jerry's wife Heather then asked: "You mean just like the one that that woman Kayla was talking about on TV last night?"

Traci Wedley nodded vigorously and then told her father: "Wow, dad, Kayla Burke is so cool. She's got like one billion followers."

"Oh, come on now," her mother told her. "This couldn't ever be that same book."

"Personally, I hope it is," Jerry said. "Cuz then we're all gonna be millionaires too!"

And the whole family had a great laugh over that.

Jerry really needed that laugh, that release of pent-up emotion. He felt very close to crazy from what he'd seen and experienced last night. He was managing his horror as well as he could.

Jerry hadn't told Heather about the murder. She'd been soundly asleep when he'd arrived home, which he'd been grateful for. He intended to let Heather learn about the gruesome death from social media. He didn't desire to relive the experience by relating it to her.

But there was only so much self-therapy that a man could do for himself, and the weird book lying there on the family breakfast table was quite the reminder that something odd had happened to him.

Jerry felt very relieved when young Traci, who was a goth type of teen and liked creepy stuff like this, took the weird book to school with her to show it to her goth friends.

But then, after Traci left for school with it, Jerry Wedley found another copy of the weird book in his pocket when he arrived at work that afternoon.

On discovering this additional copy, Jerry felt a fresh surge of terror concerning what had transpired last night.

Did that severed head in the microwave really talk to me? he asked himself yet again. *Were the cops right in assuming that I hallucinated it all, or did it actually happen?*

But then, the feeling of dread (and those accompanying terrifying questions too) passed and the world around Jerry seemed normal and rational again, although with insanity lurking just beyond its borders.

But Jerry soon began wondering exactly how many copies of the book he'd actually found last night, particularly after his wife Heather called to tell him something and then mentioned that she'd just found a copy of the little book in their kitchen, and how, if she concentrated hard enough, she could make sense of its contents.

"Traci was right, honey," Heather Wedley said. "That little book actually is titled 'How to Succeed in Life.' "

Then Heather sighed deeply, her exhaled breath rattling over the phone connection.

"Is anything the matter, hon?" Jerry asked her nervously, correctly sensing that there was something more about the book that Heather wanted to tell him.

"So, honey, I tried reading that book and it's really creepy stuff," Heather told him. "But thankfully, afterwards I couldn't remember anything of what I'd read. Not a single thing. Now, darling, is that strange, or what?"

The End

ABOUT THE AUTHOR

Wol-vriey is Nigerian, and quite tall.

He believes there actually are things that go bump in the night.

He writes horror fiction—for adults only, please. And also some surrealist stuff.

Wol-vriey blogs at: *http://oddityfarm.wordpress.com*

WOL-VRIEY
BIZARRO AND TRANSGRESSIVE FICTION

BOSTON POSH (BUD MALONE #1)

In 2028 AD, the USA is a nation ravaged by hungry dragons and dinosaurs. In Boston, Massachusetts, private eye Bud Malone is hired to rescue a kidnapped heiress. But nothing is as it seems.

Malone works to unravel a tangled web involving Boston Chinatown, a 200-year-old woman with a 9-year-old body, white robots, a human-liver-eating psychopath, a golem, a porcelain dragon, and a snake goddess with a crush on him. There's also a woman obsessed with chicken sex. Then Malone meets Posh Lane, a gorgeous call girl who's desperate to quit her pimp.

Romantic sparks ignite between Posh and Malone, but Posh's past suddenly catches up with her in a BIG way. To save Posh, Malone agrees to run a quest for Earth's new rulers, the Forks. But, Malone has no idea that agreeing to the Fork's odd request will send him on the weirdest trip he's ever been on in his life.

BOSTON CORPSE (BUD MALONE #2)

MAGIC CAN BE MURDER! - Drag queen Lucy Tang is back in Boston, and is hell-bent on settling her vindetta against casino owner Sookie Ling. And suddenly, Bud Malone, PI, has the case of his life to resolve.

When Boston's robot police force are baffled by a mind transfer case, they come to Malone for help. The one person who can likely help Malone out here is the witch Soledad Bathory. But Soledad seems to know a lot more than she's telling him. It's a case not made easier when Malone meets Soledad's beautiful cousin, Josephine 'Slave' Bailey. Slave has her own plans for Malone, most of which involve teaching him BDSM and making him her new Master.

Oh, and Rick Rogers owes Sookie Ling a whole lot of money, a gambling debt that's going to be literally Hell to pay!

BOSTON CORPSE - Not your average detective novel!

Burning Bulb
PUBLISHING

WOL-VRIEY
BIZARRO AND TRANSGRESSIVE FICTION

BOSTON LUST (BUD MALONE #3)

"Bless it, Father, for she has sinned."

Seven murdered gay women, all their bodies completely drained of blood. All also with large parts of their bodies dissolved away like acid has been pumped into their veins.

Bud Malone has to find the female vampire preying on Boston's lesbian population.

Then Malone meets the beautiful Trudi Carmen and the case gets even more tangled. Trudi needs Malone's help in recovering a ring that's gone missing. But how in the world is one little black ring related to either the dead women or their killer?

Resolving this case will lead Malone deep into Lucy Tang's legacy –the Abstracta. And then to the city of Genesis.

Boston Lust –just when you thought Bean Town was safe to visit again.

HELL DANCER

Six people find themselves trapped in Detention, a nightmare realm where the demonic Schoolmaster is hell-bent on reforming them . . . until they die.

Porn superstar Venus Deluxe came to Springfield, MA to party, and next found her life hanging by a thread. One wrong answer will mean her death.

Suspended BPD detective Tanya Rockford was trying to stop one kind of violence, but found a terrifying another. With her and her companion's lives hanging in the balance, it's going to take all of her courage and resourcefulness to escape this hell she's stumbled into.

Porn stud Chad Cannon has made a career from his ten-inch penis. Here in Detention, however, it's his brains that matter. He'll soon be hoping all the pot he's smoked over the years hasn't completely messed up his memory.

The three students, Sherri, Jordan, and Mike? They were all just in the wrong place at the right time. Will anyone survive Detention? The evil Schoolmaster doesn't plan on letting that happen . . .

Burning Bulb
PUBLISHING

WOL-VRIEY

BIZARRO AND TRANSGRESSIVE FICTION

VAGINA MUNDI

Rachel Risk is a professional thief with super-strong hair that can stretch like tentacles to manipulate objects. Ashley Status has both a digitally augmented brain, and 'muscle-purses' in her arms and legs in which she stores inflatable objects—cars, guns, rocket launchers, etc.

When Raye is framed as the fall girl in a jewel robbery, the pair flee Chicago's vengeful robot gangsters and take refuge in the Hotel Bizarre, where the gorgeous 'vagina singer,' Femina, is performing for a week.

But the Hotel Bizarre is even stranger than its name suggests, and very soon Raye and Ash are involved in an deadly adventure, a struggle for survival the likes of which they'd never imagined possible with loads of deviant sex, drugs, music, and violence at every turn. And just what is the old woman in the skin desert really doing with all those cats glued to her walls?

VAGINA MUNDI—a Bizarro Hymn in praise of WOMAN!

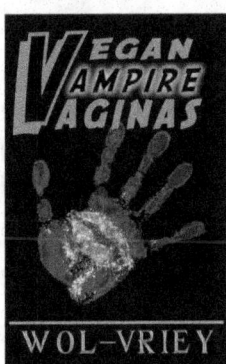

VEGAN VAMPIRE VAGINAS

The biggest bank heist in US history. And Tom Palmer can't remember pulling it off. And no, this isn't your standard case of amnesia. After a one-night-stand gone horribly wrong, Boston salesman Tom Palmer wakes up with a vagina implanted in his left hand. Then his day gets worse.

Tom is transported across space-time to a nightmare version of Boston, one where the Bizarro virus has transformed half the population into cannibals. Worst of all, Tom discovers that in this new Boston, he's the infamous gangster Pussypalm, wanted for robbing the Federal Reserve Bank of Boston a year ago. He also learns that the vagina in his hand is prophetic, i.e. it talks . . . after sex.

With 130 people left dead during his bank heist and six billion dollars missing, Tom knows he's living on borrowed time. It is in his best interests not to remember anything. Because once he does . .

Burning Bulb

WOL-VRIEY
BIZARRO AND TRANSGRESSIVE FICTION

VEGAN ZOMBIE APOCALYPSE

In the post-apocalypse worlderness, zombies rule the earth. They're allergic to meat, and brains literally make them explode. Zombies now eat blood potatoes, parasitic tubers grown in the flesh of humancows corralled in maximum security farms. Two fugitives meet in the ancient ruins of Texas. The first is Soil 15-f, a womancow who's escaped her farm a week before she's due to be killed and her blood potato crop harvested. The second fugitive is Able Kane, former head necros food technician, now sentenced to death for heresy. But Soil is no ordinary humancow.

Unknown to herself, she's the vegan zombie agricultural revolution, and the zombies desperately want her back. And the necros equally desperately want Able Kane dead. He's fled with a forbidden discovery which will reshape the world for the worse if used. And Able is just hardheaded/misguided enough to use it.

MELANIE NEMESIS CATCHPOLE

In Springfield, Massachusetts, Melanie Catchpole is hired to fetch back a magic teddy bear worth millions of dollars from a warehouse across town. Problem is, the warehouse is down in Springfield's O-Zone that totally weird sector of the city where Bizarro fell to Earth. The 'O' is a fairytale land, a place where dreams and nightmares literally live and breathe..

Worse still, the gingers—mutant cannibals—prowl the O. The gingers have already eaten everyone else Melanie's employers sent to get back the magic teddy bear.

Accompanied by the handsome but ruthless Doug Fisher (who she finds sexy but doesn't dare entrust her heart to), Melanie enters the O-Zone. Melanie and Doug are instantly caught up in an adventure they'd never have believed credible even if written as fiction . . . and Melanie's used to experiencing the very weird as the norm.

And now, additionally, there's a mystery to unravel: What does the dark, freezing-cold being called The Fixer want with Mary, the barkeep's daughter?

Burning Bulb
PUBLISHING

WOL-VRIEY
BIZARRO AND TRANSGRESSIVE FICTION

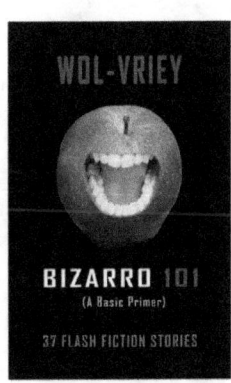

BIG TROUBLE IN LITTLE ASS

From Bizarro master storyteller Wol-vriey comes a truly weird western tale that will leave you awe-struck and on the edge of your seat...

In the town named Little Ass, tight-assed prostitute Rosa overhears a gunslinger's plans to assassinate rancher Edison Bennett. Once the badass Bennett learns of the plot, he ensures there'll be hell to pay for any attempt on his life!

Yes, it's going to take all of gunslinger Jude's shooting prowess, his eclectic collection of strange firearms, a trusty horse that requires an owners' manual, and the help of the lovely and invigorating Nell (who's EXTREMELY odd when the going gets weird), to survive the Bizarro hell that Edison Bennett unleashes in order to hold onto the land that he'd stolen from Madam Zizi.

BIZARRO 101 (A BASIC PRIMER)

Welcome to the strange place:

A collection of 37 flash fiction stories designed to introduce one to the Bizarro/New Weird Genre.

Weird, dreamy, nightmarish, absurd, sad, surreal, humorous . . . this collection of tales is all this and more.

***

"This primer is the very essence of any and all styles and types of Bizarro writing. Wol-vriey collects, distills, and bottles up these 37 tiny stories for your sensory enjoyment. This is an absolute must-read for anyone new to the genre, because it demonstrates the scope of what Bizarro is, and what it can be."
         –Teresa Pollack, Bizarro commentator and blogger

Burning Bulb
PUBLISHING

WOL-VRIEY
BIZARRO AND TRANSGRESSIVE FICTION

Dr. Orgasm

Courtney Taylor is young, intelligent, beautiful, and successful. She also has a boyfriend who loves her deeply. The problem is, no matter what Courtney does, she can't climax during sex.

When Florence Rigid's communist forces destroy the city of Metaphor, Courtney and her friends Teresa, Highball, Miki, and Heather are cast into the midst of a quest to find the only person able to save the land of Innuendo—Dr. Carol Orgasm, wanted by the communists for developing the O-Pill, a wonder drug that grants women sexual ecstasy on demand.

The communists will do anything to get their hands on the O-Pill and prevent its reaching the millions of Innuendo's women. But Courtney desperately wants that pill too. And so it's now a race between Courtney and the communists to find Dr. Orgasm first.

And Courtney has no choice but to win this race. She must win it: For her own orgasm . . . and for the freedom of female sexuality everywhere.

PUSSY TRANSMISSION

Pussy Transmission were the most decadent Pop Art ensemble of the 90's. Led by the beautiful painter Isis Lynch, the trio revolutionized the art world. Then suddenly, without explanation, Pussy Transmission vanished into historical obscurity. Now, twenty years later, three women come to Lynch Place. Lily and Nina are journalists desperate to interview Isis Lynch. Raven, on the other hand, wants to find her boyfriend, who's gone missing inside Isis's house. Raven's worried—she's heard that Pussy Transmission broke up because Isis began dabbling in black magic . . . with devastating results. All three women will shortly wish they'd never left home. Particularly once the rats in Lynch Place start warning them that they're going to die . . . and Raven meets Betty Butcher, the bouncy supernatural psycho who's intent on chopping her into bits. Pussy Transmission, Baby! Just because . . .

Burning Bulb

WOL-VRIEY
BIZARRO AND TRANSGRESSIVE FICTION

GIRLS ARE NOT SMILING

Welcome To The Road Trip From Hell

Pagan is demon-possessed.

Lori is suicidal.

Britt is just terminally pissed off.

Meet three young Boston women on the run from the law, each with problems that will fuse into more than the sum of their individual parts, becoming a holocaust of sex and violence and terror, a literal rain of blood and horror and gore and evil.

And if that wasn't already bad enough, Pagan's pet demon is slowly transforming her into something both unspeakable and unholy. Truly, these girls aren't smiling.

BLUE NIGHTMARES

Consummate EVIL is coming. It is relentless and unavoidable. It is Blue.

Jessica Schreiber is seeing things. Very horrible things. Since arriving in Raynham for what should have been a relaxing vacation, she's been seeing *The Big Blue*.

Jessica is smelling things too—dead and rotting things that she can't see. She is sure those dead and rotting things are dead people. Lots of dead people.

Jessica's worst nightmares will soon become her reality. Her reality will soon become a terrifying nightmare.

The tentacled residents of the House of Death have a lot that they wish to show Jessica Schreiber. They have a lot that they wish to tell her. But will she survive long enough to learn their lessons?

Burning Bulb
PUBLISHING

WOL-VRIEY
BIZARRO AND TRANSGRESSIVE FICTION

BRAINCHEW

It was supposed to be a simple jewel heist, but it went badly wrong. Chuck got shot and died.

Lance hid his friend's corpse in the Pleasant Street Cemetery. But that was a big mistake—there was something undead, something extremely hungry . . . something eXXXtremely horrible, buried in the Pleasant Street Cemetery.

And Lance had just woken it up.

They called the monster Brainchew because it ate brains. Human brains. And it preferred those brains fresh from the heads . . . of the living.

And now it was awake again, Brainchew planned on feeding big-time tonight. Oh hell yes, it did.

BRAINCHEW 2: OUT OF THEIR HEADS

After Tiff Hooper recognizes Josh Penham, the man who abducted her and kept her in his basement and abused her, she brings her three friends to Raynham for a night of well-deserved revenge on him.

Only things don't go according to plan.

It is never a good idea to leave a corpse in Raynham's Pleasant Street Cemetery. You run the very real risk of awakening what lies underground there. And that thing—Brainchew—is more horrible and more evil than anything the average mind conceives of even in its worst nightmares.

Brainchew is back! And this time the monster is extra-hungry. But there are plenty of delicious human brains about tonight, and Brainchew intends to eat them all before dawn.

Burning Bulb

WOL-VRIEY
BIZARRO AND TRANSGRESSIVE FICTION

DARIA: AN EROTIC NIGHTMARE

Even the best laid women can go wrong.

Daria Simpson is HUNGRY. She's HUNGRY for sex and bloodshed and death.

Shelly Parker just wanted to have a threesome with her boyfriend Craig and her best friend Erica. Everything was shaping up nicely for their weekend of sexual fun and games, until they stopped at the creepy Crossway Diner and met Daria.

From the moment they met Daria, EVERYTHING went wrong for them; and it went wrong in the most horrific and terrifying of ways!

Daria: Paranormal service has been resumed.

WET BONES

Greg is about learning the hard way that you don't mess with Aunt Grace.

Nine completely fleshless skeletons recovered in the Massachusetts woods. Two detectives on the trail of a horrible, hungry monster.

Broken-hearted Allie Jackson has a date with a creature from Hell.

Things are about to get well out of hand for everyone, and in horrifying, terrifying ways they don't expect.

Burning Bulb

WOL-VRIEY
BIZARRO AND TRANSGRESSIVE FICTION

MR. UGLY

When a rotting corpse appears and starts butchering Raynham's youths, there's really only one question that needs answering:

Is this faceless and rotting monster Peter Howard, or isn't it?

Problem is, Peter Howard died 15 years ago. So how can he possibly be back from the dead and murdering people with such relentless and incredible brutality?

Peter's mother Malicia, who's just been released from the lunatic asylum may have the answers to the crazy puzzle, but the two detectives investigating the deaths don't even know the right questions to ask her yet.

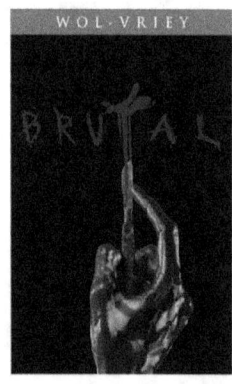

BRUTAL

Jane Winters is 28 years old.

She works as a checkout cashier in a department store. She's an attractive woman with a winning personality. She has both a photographic memory and an I.Q. of 189.

She's met the man of her dreams.

But she's also a cannibal with a unique and very scary mode of operation.

The group known as TULIP (The Urban Legend Investigation People) are out to either prove or disprove the legend of Insane Jane.

But have TULIP bitten off more than they can chew?

Burning Bulb
PUBLISHING

WOL-VRIEY
BIZARRO AND TRANSGRESSIVE FICTION

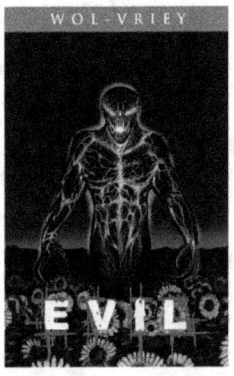

EVIL

The Evil began the week before Sylvia Stewart's 30th birthday.

Cathy Higgins died.

The Bargainer resurrected Cathy . . . for a price.

The price? Cathy's father Ronan had to plant some seeds for him.

But these were no ordinary seeds the Bargainer gave to Ronan Higgins. These were seeds from Hell: seeds which required human flesh as both soil and fertilizer.

And meanwhile, the unsuspecting Sylvia Stewart went ahead with the plans for her birthday party, which was to be held on Ronan Higgins' sunflower farm . . .

666

Ohio's State Route 666 stretches 14.7 miles between Zanesville and Dresden.

Most days, it's just a normal road with a funny name.

But for six minutes on the 6th of June each year, Route 666 becomes a gateway to somewhere else . . . a gateway to Hell.

Each year 13 unfortunates get trapped in the 666 underworld, with no way to get back home.

This year though, things are going to be very different. For one thing, there are currently a whole lot of turbulent human emotions at play in the underworld. And also . . . the psycho Al Gore is just about completing his collection of human heads.

And . . . what the hell is a church doing in Hell, of all places?

Burning Bulb
PUBLISHING

WOL-VRIEY
BIZARRO AND TRANSGRESSIVE FICTION

THE CLEAVERMAN

It began as a joke, a gag to pass the time that turned deadly. One rainy August night in Raynham, MA, nine friends jokingly invoke the evil phantom butcher called the Cleaverman.

These nine friends get a whole lot more than they ever bargained for. Because there's only one way to return the deadly Cleaverman back to the darkness he came from, and that is to solve his riddle, which starts: "Tell me the name of John Cleaverman's wife . . ."

And human beings being what we are, even with the Cleaverman out to butcher them all, our nine friends still manage to stir A WHOLE LOT of human misbehavior into the deadly mix.

At the rate they're going, it'll be a wonder if anyone survives THE CLEAVERMAN at all.

PERVERSE

When 21-year-old Heather Forrest accompanies three of her friends on a weekend trip up to Vermont, she has no idea what she's getting into.

Because, during a brief stop in the western Massachusetts woods, the girls get kidnapped and things go rapidly downhill from there. Soon Heather and her friends are fighting for their lives, fighting to survive the most perverted and impossible situation imaginable. And meanwhile, Hank Rollins is also in the woods, hunting the unholy monster that killed his wife and son . . . and he's hunting it with live human bait.

Oh yes, there will be blood. And there will be terror and buckets of gore also. And truly horrible atrocities will happen. Most definitely so.

Burning Bulb

WOL-VRIEY
BIZARRO AND TRANSGRESSIVE FICTION

THE VIRGIN

10 million dollars in prize money. 1000+ video cameras, lots of deadly weapons, 10 Suitors, 5 Virgins & 3 Hours . . . to keep your hymen intact.

Hailey Osborne wants to sell her virginity for a hundred thousand dollars. But then she's made an offer she really can't refuse: how about competing to win ten million dollars in a no-holds-barred underground game show, where all she has to do is remain a virgin?

There's just two problems:
1. Four other women also want that prize money.
2. There's ten suitors all contesting to take Hailey and the other virgins' precious hymens . . . by any means necessary . . .

But hey, it's just for 3 hours, right? How hard can it possibly be ? Hailey Osborne is about to find out.

THE BOOK OF ATROCITIES

Bestselling author Drake Melville has been missing for three years now. Drake vanished after publishing The Bleeding Oysters, an epic novel that set new standards for depictions of sleaze and depravity and human monstrosity in popular fiction. On vanishing, however, Drake Melville left a message for everyone, saying he'd 'left town' to go work on his follow-up novel The Book of Atrocities. The problem was, no one could find Drake. It seemed like he'd vanished off the face of the Earth. And now, three years later, Drake has just sent messages to his ex-wife Liz, his current (and abandoned) wife Melody; and his younger sister Chloe . . . asking them to meet him in Raynham, MA. Drake says he's now completed The Book of Atrocities and is ready to present it to the world. But there's a whole lot that Liz, Melody, and Chloe Melville don't know about Drake's Book of Atrocities. And unfortunately they're on their way to find out those excruciatingly painful truths. Because, see, Drake Melville is a VERY EVIL man with a VERY EVIL plan . . .

Burning Bulb

WOL-VRIEY
BIZARRO AND TRANSGRESSIVE FICTION

THE FINAL GIRL

Here there be monsters . . . because we made them.

At a secret location, 8 young women assemble to compete on the ultimate reality/game show—The Final Girl. The 8 contestants are: A young wife and her grown-up stepdaughter, a police detective, a prostitute, a nurse, a school teacher, and unemployed twin sisters.

The Final Girl is a no-holds-barred show beamed to an audience on the Dark Web, a show where murder is permitted and mutilation is encouraged.

The Rules:
1. Avoid being killed and eaten by the show's monsters and bogeymen.
2. Find the prize money—24 million dollars in cash.
3. Hold on to the money.

But only 1 woman can win. And to win The Final Girl reality show, that woman will need to be even more bloodthirsty and ruthless than the show's monsters.

Have a seat, everyone. The most dangerous game is about to begin!

WOMEN

John Miller must die . . . TONIGHT!

Megan Kemp initially went to the Penderson Mansion to collect a debt. But from the moment she stepped in there, getting back outside proved extremely difficult. And then what had merely been difficult for Megan suddenly turned deadly. Because something was going on in the Penderson Mansion that night. Five VERY ANGRY women had a score to settle, and no obstacle on earth would stop them. . . . And no one would get in their way and live to tell the tale either. "John Miller must die," the women had decreed, and it looked like the forces of Hell would help them accomplish their deadly aim tonight.

But as the night progressed, Megan, who was now trapped in a deadly game of cat and mouse in the Penderson Mansion, found that despite her own troubles, her biggest question was: "What the hell did John Miller do to anger these five women this much?"

Beware, folks . . . sometimes things really do go too far!

Burning Bulb

WOL-VRIEY
BIZARRO AND TRANSGRESSIVE FICTION

RATIO OF BROOKES TO ASHLEYS

After being cursed by a dying woman, Mike Broadman's love life completely nosedives. One girlfriend cheats on him and the next one dies a very messy death.

Next, a psychic informs Mike that he's under an evil spell that will keep killing his girlfriends, and that the ONLY solution (the ONLY way that he'll ever have a happy love life again) is for him to only date women named either Brooke or Ashley from now on.

Mike tries to comply with this, but still, the deaths continue, and now they're becoming even more brutal and bloody. Mike now finds himself in a race against time. He needs to 'equalize the ratio of Brookes to Ashleys' before it's too late.

And then, just when it seems things can't get any crazier or deadlier for Mike, he meets 'Brash' — the twins Brooke and Ashley Lawrence . . .

And the body count keeps rising . . .

DELICIOUS ZOMBIE

The zombie apocalypse happened two years ago. Today, zombies are mankind's new cattle. The undead are headed like cows and killed and eaten by everyone. The reason for this atrocity? Eating zombie meat has been scientifically proven to reverse human aging. Therefore, anyone who eats the zombies will live forever. Nowadays there are no old people anywhere on Earth. Everyone is young and healthy. Even deadly diseases have regressed. "

Digestion is Salvation," the Church of Zombie preaches. But three people—scientist Ethan Hackman, ex CIA assassin Paula Neyman, and socialite Zoe Patterson—seek to change this madness that is modern life.

With a group of ruthless and sadistic bounty hunters hot on their trail as they attempt to save the world, will Ethan, Paula, and Zoe succeed in curing the zombies, or will the age of the 'Delicious Zombie' continue? One thing is for certain, however; there will be a HUGE amount of murder and mutilation, bloodshed, violence and gore before the knotty issue of the zombies' food status is resolved.

Burning Bulb

WOL-VRIEY
BIZARRO AND TRANSGRESSIVE FICTION

MOTEL GOTHIC

The Devil's Coin Game was a game for desperate men. And Dooks, Hicks, and Robby were three such men, men with nothing to lose, men prepared to gamble their lives away on the flip of a coin. The rules of the game were simple: one man would die, the other two would have their wishes granted by the devil. At midnight in the Sunflower Motel, the Devil's Coin Game will be played, and one of the players will not survive.

Elsewhere in the Sunflower Motel, two female assassins Mandy Cherry and Dewdrop arrive to murder someone. But things are guaranteed to go awry when the intended victim is a witch.

And on this same portentous night, Roman is about to have an unforgettable meeting with a prostitute named Christine. Christine Valona supposedly brings bad luck to all those who encounter her; but why is this, and who is she?

THE BACHELOR

One eligible bachelor, thirteen gorgeous young women, and a TV crew, on a remote Pacific island paradise. What could possibly go wrong? A lot!

Tired of his refusal to get married and make her some grandchildren, American playboy Tyler Bradley is given a 90-day ultimatum by his wealthy mother to either get married or be disowned.

As a solution, Tyler's best friend, TV producer Disney Dizzford suggests that they hold a 'bachelor-seeking-love' themed reality show on Eternity Island, a remote island paradise off of the coast of Guatemala, which for some reason the Guatemalan government pretends doesn't exist. "When the black cloud comes," the strange old man warned, "monsters will emerge from the sea. When the black cloud covers the sky, all will die."

But nobody takes the old guy seriously, because of course this is the 21st century and there are no such things as sea monsters, right? That sort of stuff only happens in bad movies, right?

Wrong. The black cloud just arrived over Eternity Island . . .

Burning Bulb

WOL-VRIEY
BIZARRO AND TRANSGRESSIVE FICTION

MARRIAGE

Adam Norwood, suffering from an extreme photosensitivity skin condition, resides on a secluded island with his wife, Phoebe, and his possible wizard of a father-in-law, Lester. Despite outward appearances of a happy marriage, Adam's life is plagued by recurring nightmares in which Phoebe repeatedly kills him, driving him to the brink of insanity. To add to his woes, Hilary Burton, an alluring party guest on Goat Island, mistakenly identifies Adam as her former lover and is determined to win him back, setting the stage for a calamity that threatens the lives of everyone on the island.

Adam's condition and nightmarish visions pale in comparison to the impending peril he's about to face. The arrival of Hilary Burton unravels a sinister chain of events that may jeopardize the very existence of the island's residents, pushing Adam to discover a new and dire meaning of "bad" and "deadly."

THE MAN WHO KILLED HIS WIFE

Maryanne Wilson's death was definitely an accident. Her husband Bob had absolutely no intention of killing her.

But it was almost certain that a court of law would see things differently, particularly after Bob had sex with Maryanne's corpse . . . and that was why Bob Wilson decided not to call in the police, but to seek an alternative solution to the problem he'd gotten himself into . . . A solution which unfortunately only made matters a whole lot worse for him.

Everything began because Bob Wilson was working too hard and as a result was neglecting his loving wife, Maryanne.

And so, Maryanne asked their upstairs neighbor Jennifer for help.

Jennifer Haskins apparently knew a little magic, and so she cast a spell on Bob, one that would help Maryanne get laid on a more regular basis, like every night if she so desired.

What could possibly go wrong with a simple arrangement like that? Everything you can't possibly imagine . . .

Burning Bulb

WOL-VRIEY
BIZARRO AND TRANSGRESSIVE FICTION

LGBT: LUST, GORE, BLOODSHED, & TERROR

Hey, you want something completely effed up? Well, here it is! LUST: Lavelle, the lesbian porno actress whose dead lover comes back as a ghost to haunt her. GORE: Greg, the elderly gay man who decides to butcher his young, unfaithful husband and his husband's boyfriend. BLOODSHED: Bryn, the bisexual vampire endlessly seeking her soulmate, but who, somehow, always ends up killing her lovers. TERROR: Tammi, the disgraced transgender influencer who, unable to afford the cost of her Gender Affirmation Surgery, decides to become a 'complete woman' by magical means. These four people meet and interact at the Bonner's Corner nightclub, where their intersecting schemes and dreams will place them on a series of collision courses with each other that will lead to weird consequences for some and horrifying ends for others. Oh, and the witch named Rainbow. Why is Rainbow called 'Rainbow' anyway?

NIGHTMARE FUEL

After Dustin's girlfriend breaks up with him, his new neighbors introduce him to the Real Dreams club to help him get over the breakup. But the Real Dreams club is much stranger than it appears. While on the surface, Real Dreams appears to be a members-only sex club, everything at Real Dreams is fueled by the hallucinogenic drink called Nightmare Fuel, or *Nif* for short. Under *Nif's* strange influence, sex, torture, and murder are merely the tip of an iceberg of depravity, an insane debauched whirlwind that revolves around the worship of the worm goddess Boku Veeza. What exactly has Dustin gotten himself into? Because the longer he remains at the club, the crazier his life becomes. Dustin knows that the Real Dreams club members are keeping a huge secret from him. But can he learn what their secret is and save himself from the unsuspected and unholy terrors of . . . NIGHTMARE FUEL?

Burning Bulb
PUBLISHING

www.ingramcontent.com/pod-product-compliance
Lightning Source LLC
Chambersburg PA
CBHW070014260626
47159CB00005B/1804